N E LINCS LIBRARIES

5 4073 00958627 4

Butterfly Soup

A Novel

Jan Marsh

NORTH EAST LINCOLNSHIRE LIBRARIES

WITHDRAWN FROM STOCK

NORTH EAST LINCOLNSHIRE LIBRARIES

9/10

D1477253

CLE

GCB

GCL

NORTH EAST
LINCOLNSHIRE
LIBRARIES

WIL

YAR

ROUTE:

NORTH EAST LINCOLNSHIRE COUNCIL

00958627	
Bertrams	24/06/2010
CRI	£8.99

Published 2010 by Onlywomen Press Ltd., London, UK

ISBN 978-0-9561053-1-8 (paperback)

British Library Cataloguing-in-Publication Data
A catalogue record for this book is available from the British Library

Copyright © Jan Marsh 2010

The moral right of Jan Marsh to be identified as the author of this work has
been asserted in accordance with the Copyright, Design and Patents Act, 1988.

All rights reserved.

No part of this publication may be reproduced or transmitted in any form or
by any means, electronic or mechanical, including photocopy, recording, or
any information storage and retrieval system without permission in writing
from the publisher.

Cover Design © Spark, 2009
Typeset by FiSH Books, Enfield
Printed in the UK by CPI Mackays, Chatham, ME5 8TD

This book is sold subject to the condition that it will not, by trade or
otherwise, be lent, re-sold, hired out or otherwise circulated without the
publisher's prior written consent in any form of binding or cover than that in
which it is published here and without a similar condition being imposed on
the subsequent purchaser.

Except for short passages for review purposes no part of this publication may
be reproduced, stored in a retrieval system or transmitted in any form, or by
any means, electronic, mechanical, photocopying, recording or otherwise
without the prior written permission of Onlywomen Press, Ltd.

Chapter One

Just for once, thought Gabrielle, as she pulled up in the quiet cul de sac and let her battered Toyota shudder into silence, I would like to care about another human being without having to examine my conscience.

But as she got out of her car and walked towards the house, she continued to argue with herself. Should she really be here? Gabrielle shut her mind to further analysis and opened the gate.

She walked up the path to the sliding glass door. She knocked twice and tried not to peer in but she couldn't help noticing the two-seater couch on one side of the room and a dining-table with two upright chairs on the other. It was no surprise to Gabrielle that the room was neat to the point of sterility. So neat, in fact, that the large pair of trainers, sole-uppermost, in the corner, looked very out of place. She waited, but there was no sound inside. She knocked again. Nothing.

As she turned to leave she noticed that the trainers were attached to trousers. She stared hard through the glass door. Someone lay face-down at the far side of the room, their dark clothes almost blending in with the brown carpet. She tried the handle, and the door slid smoothly aside. With her heart trying to escape through her rib-cage and every instinct screaming 'no!' she stepped over the threshold.

A man lay in the hall doorway, like a toppled tin soldier. One arm was twisted behind him and a stain had darkened the carpet around him.

Gabrielle took a gulp of air. She choked on the foul smell. She went closer but couldn't bring herself to touch him. His hair was a ring of grey stubble like a monk's tonsure, he was wearing a mud-coloured track suit and, apart from the stain on the carpet, he looked unharmed. His head pointed the way to the bedroom, which was as neat as the living-room.

Gabrielle wondered briefly if she should check the man's pulse, maybe try to resuscitate him, but even as she thought of this she was backing towards the door. She knew the smell of death. Often on the farm there would be a dead sheep in a gully or creek and even a day or two was enough for the sickly smell to develop. She resorted to a gesture she hadn't used since she left home: she crossed herself, then turned and ran out the door and down the path. Safely outside the gate, she scrambled through her bag for her cellphone and dialled the police. Then she sat in her car, staring ahead.

Sirens cut the air. The ambulance arrived first and Gabrielle waved the paramedics towards the sliding door. The police pulled up as the medics came out and one of the young men in St John's Ambulance uniform leaned down to speak to them through the car window.

The other walked up to Gabrielle who hovered anxiously near the gate.

'You found him?'

She nodded.

'Are you ok?' He reached for her wrist and held it for a moment. His hand felt comforting. 'Your pulse is a bit fast. You might be in shock. Take it easy for the rest of the day won't you?'

She nodded again. Her tongue could not seem to form words.

The ambulance drove off, silent and empty.

The police officers, a man and a woman, got out of their car and went up to Gabrielle, who swallowed hard and forced herself to speak.

'It was me who called,' she said. 'He's dead isn't he?'

The woman nodded. 'The ambulance officers said so. We'll have a look, wait here.'

They stepped through the door but came out almost immediately. The man talked into the radio attached to his jacket. The woman came over to Gabrielle. Her uniform made her look bulky but Gabrielle could see that she was muscular rather than heavy and underneath the no-nonsense haircut her face was kind.

'Do you know who he is?' she asked.

'No. My client lives here, a young woman.'

'Client?'

'I'm a counsellor. Jasmine didn't come to her appointment so I called round to see if she was all right. The door was open...' Gabrielle covered her mouth with her hand. She felt sick thinking about the toppled form inside.

The man turned from his radio and spoke to his partner. 'The detectives are on their way.' Turning to Gabrielle he asked, 'Who are you?'

'Gabrielle Murphy.'

'Did you touch anything?'

She shook her head.

'We'll need a statement.'

Gabrielle was taken aback by his abrupt manner. The woman seemed to realise that and spoke more gently. 'Can you drive ok?'

Gabrielle nodded.

'Good, then come down to the station and we'll go over what happened. Ask for me, I'm Carol.' She handed Gabrielle a card.

When she got into her car Gabrielle felt her heart racing. She wanted to cry, but not in front of the police who seemed so stern and in control. She drove slowly down the street and round the corner where she stopped and let the tears come, flowing from her own shock and also from fear that something bad had happened to Jasmine. After a while, she started the car and went to the police station, arriving ahead of Carol. As she sat in the waiting room, she studied the posters: 'Lock it or lose it' 'If you drink and then drive you're bloody idiot'. There weren't any about finding a body.

Carol arrived and used a card to open the side door. She showed Gabrielle into a plain room with a table and chairs and left her sitting there while she went to get them some tea. She came back with a polystyrene cup in each hand and Gabrielle took one gratefully. A middle-aged man in a jacket and tie followed Carol into the room. He had the tanned, tweedy look of one of her father's friends at a stock sale and a lined face which had seen it all.

He shook her hand. '° Walt Parker.'

He and Carol sat at the table opposite Gabrielle. For a moment it was as if she was observing herself in a TV crime serial.

'Tell us what happened,' he said.

It felt like an invitation to open the flood-gates and Gabrielle could feel the tears pricking her eyes but she wanted to tell the story calmly, professionally. She sipped the hot tea while she gathered her thoughts.

'My client, Jasmine Lawson, lives there. She's usually very reliable about her appointments so when she didn't turn up I was worried. When I was finished for the day I thought I'd just pop round with another appointment for her.'

Carol looked up from her note-taking. 'You didn't phone?'

'She doesn't have a phone – too expensive to get it connected she said. Maybe she has a cellphone but she didn't give me the number.'

'Would you normally call in on a client who didn't turn up?' asked Parker.

'Well, no, but I know she lives alone and I thought what if she's sick. I decided no daughter of mine should lie ill in bed with no one to care about her, so...'

'Daughter?' Parker cut in.

Gabrielle blushed. 'I mean client.' She lost her train of thought as she pictured what her supervisor would make of the Freudian slip.

Parker made the connection. 'So she's more special than your other clients.' He didn't seem to be asking.

Gabrielle sighed. 'I was struggling with that a bit myself. She's kind of vulnerable but gutsy – tries to make the best of a hard life. But anyway, I had no other way to get in touch and I thought if she wasn't there I'd just put the card in the letter box.'

'And then...'

'I knocked and there was no answer and I was just about to leave when I saw there was someone lying on the floor. I guess it was instinctive to see if he was all right and the door was unlocked. But I knew as soon as I went in ... the smell ... I came straight out and phoned emergency services.'

There was a knock at the door and the male officer put his head in to speak to the detective. While they talked in low voices in the hall-way Carol asked about Gabrielle's work.

'I've been a counsellor for about five years now. I used to work at the Women's Centre but now I work from home. Not just with women, I see all kinds of clients, couples as well. I've been busy enough these last two years to make a living without any other work.'

Parker beckoned Carol over to the door and said quietly, 'It is Don Lawson. When did he get out?'

'About a month ago,' she said. 'Must have got the notification when you were on leave. But I thought he was on parole in Christchurch. He's not supposed to be here.'

'Do we know where his victims are?'

'I can get addresses from the file. The main lad would have left school by now but his mother will know where he is.'

Gabrielle tried to look as if she wasn't listening but she was inter-ested. She knew the case – didn't everyone? It must have been at least seven years ago, while she was still a receptionist in a law office, that the story had rocked the town. One after the other, young boys came forward to disclose that they had been sexually abused by the owner of the corner store. He'd got away with it for years, bribing them with cigarettes and alcohol to keep quiet. In the end, he made the mistake of molesting a non-smoker whose mother was alert enough to see her son's distress, and Don's poisonous web unravelled. The boys had said they had been filmed and there was talk of a porn ring but although Don had a video camera, no sign of tapes or a computer had been found. The police had concluded the camera was all part of Don's game to get the boys involved by pretending they were actors in a movie.

The trial was followed closely as it used all the latest techniques of evidential interviewing and closed circuit television to help the boys to speak out. Lobbyists advocated bringing back the death penalty while a few brave souls claimed that love between men and boys was natural and took place in all the great cultures. Psychologists were trotted out to give expert opinions on television, and radio talk-back ran hot. In the end Don Lawson was jailed for ten years, not long enough time to satisfy those bent on vengeance.

Gabrielle knew this through the media accounts at the time, and through the talk in the lawyers' office, but recently she had had a more intimate insight into the story.

Don Lawson was Jasmine's father.

Parker said a few words to the officer in the corridor and turned back to Gabrielle.

'The constable will take your statement down. No plans to leave town in the next few days?' Gabrielle shook her head. 'We may need to be in touch.'

He left the room and Carol turned to a fresh page of her notebook. They went through the story again as Carol wrote it down word for word.

At last the statement was finished but the non-committal way Carol heard it left Gabrielle feeling guilty, even more so when they took her fingerprints 'for elimination purposes'. Finally she was allowed to go home. She felt ridiculously grateful to be freed.

The Toyota clattered into the driveway and Gabrielle went straight to the kitchen to switch on the kettle for coffee. As she waited for the water to boil she looked around the room, trying to ground herself. The last rays of the sun threw a dappled light which made the wooden table glow like golden syrup. She breathed in the smell of the coffee as she spooned it into the plunger. Out in the garden, a fantail flicked in and out of the twigs of the apple tree and made its cork-on-bottle squeak. A few brown leaves fell to the ground, mimicking the fantail's fluttering flight. Everything looked so normal, so ordinary.

The upturned trainers projected themselves into Gabrielle's mind. To block them out, she stared hard out the window at the garden. Looking at the last few apples on the tree and the falling leaves she thought: it will soon be time to prune that tree. She pictured getting out in the garden on the weekend, raking up leaves for the compost and maybe putting in some pansies where she could see them from the kitchen. The thought of striding about in gumboots and getting her hands into the cool damp soil would normally make her happy and Autumn was her favourite season. But the idea of digging suddenly made her think of a grave and there she was back again, picturing the dead man on the floor of Jasmine's flat, his blood staining the carpet. She felt bile rise in her throat, and she sat heavily at the table, putting her head in her hands as the room began to spin. If it was a TV thriller she would have watched, cosy in her armchair with a glass of wine, just for the fun of working out who did it. But she was no observer: she'd broken a small, unimportant rule and now she was a player in a storyline that she really didn't want to see unfold.

When the floor had steadied under her, Gabrielle poured her coffee and took it across the hallway to her office. Jasmine's file was on her desk ready for her appointment, but the chair, placed carefully so that each client had a view of the garden, had remained empty. Gabrielle could picture how the young woman, still in her teens, would sit there with a cushion on her lap for comfort or protection. Most of the time she hung her head so that a swatch of blonde hair hid her face and only rarely did she make eye contact.

Flicking through the file, Gabrielle looked for any references to Jasmine's father. She found one, in the fourth session.

'J. used the cushion to enact her anger and hatred of her father, punching it and addressing him: "I hate you, I could kill you." Murderous rage and its role in healing discussed. Fear of regressing to powerlessness outside the session. A transitional object offered, J. chose a white stone – for purity? – as a reminder of her power. Next appointment 1 week.'

Gabrielle remembered that session well. She had asked about Jasmine's father and had been surprised at the young girl's vehemence. Her anger was about her father going to prison – she had always denied that he abused her, though Gabrielle had her doubts. Jasmine was only a child when the case broke open and from that time her life had changed. From a prosperous, hard-working family with a role in the local community, Jasmine, her mother and her older sister Susi had become outcasts. They had to sell the shop because they were sitting targets for graffiti and verbal expressions of disgust from the locals. Susi had left home and moved to Auckland where she said she was modelling – Jasmine suspected she was working as a prostitute. Mum took to adding brandy to her tea and retreated to a soft-focus world which did not include Jasmine.

From the age of ten Jasmine brought herself up and tried to look after her mother as well. On her seventeenth birthday she took an over-dose of her mother's tranquillisers. When their patient had finished spitting up charcoal in the Emergency Department, the staff called Gabrielle and for the past three months she had seen Jasmine every week. Even so, it seemed early days in terms of helping her to deal with her trauma. The hospital social worker had made the biggest difference so far by finding Jasmine a little flat and making sure that her mother went to Alcoholics Anonymous.

Gabrielle looked back at the file. She remembered how that session had ended. From the low table beside her, Gabrielle had picked up a small basket of polished stones and held it out to Jasmine.

'Here, take one of these to remind you of your strength.'

Jasmine had taken the basket. The stones shone, blue, pink, amber and white. She stirred them gently. She chose a large oval white one and closed her fist around it.

'Take it with you, keep it in your pocket and remember your power.' Then it was time to change the pace and direct Jasmine back into the world. 'What are you going to do now? You've worked hard this session, is there something you'd like to do to give yourself a treat?'

Jasmine thought for a moment. 'I could go to the beach and walk in the sea.'

Gabrielle nodded. 'That's a great idea. Feel the sand and the water, have some quiet time to get things into perspective.' She stood up. 'Same time next week?'

Jasmine nodded. Gabrielle had said, 'Take care,' as she left the room.

She had watched Jasmine going down the path, smiling as the young woman picked a sprig of lavender from the garden and sniffed it, then put both the lavender and the stone into her pocket and let herself out through the gate. Gabrielle remembered the affection she had felt then for her client, the respect she had for her courage and her pain.

Gabrielle read the file entry again and a shocking thought occurred to her. The notes showed that Jasmine had a motive, a wish even, to kill her father and they would be incriminating if the police got hold of them. She carefully tore out the page with the fourth session on it and slid it under some stationery in the bottom drawer of her desk.

Then the thought went a step further: Don was fresh out of prison and in Jasmine's flat. Gabrielle pictured Don turning up unannounced to demand a place to stay. Jasmine would surely have panicked.

What Gabrielle wanted most right now was to pour out the whole story to her best friend, Kathy. Something held her back from picking up the phone. She remembered her favourite quote from childhood Bible study: 'be wise as serpents and gentle as doves'. It meant be smart, think carefully and act righteously.

Chapter Two

Gabrielle woke, alert. She listened into the darkness and heard again the sound that had penetrated her sleep: a faint clank just outside the window. It seemed familiar but out of context. She kept listening. A soft rustling and again the clank, even fainter. Then nothing. Just a hedgehog, she thought, and turned over, exhausted. She tossed and turned, seeing in too-vivid detail the body on the floor.

In her dream she was running and hiding while a shadowy figure stalked her. She crawled through putrid ooze on her belly and wriggled under the foundations of a house which might have been her own but was dark and derelict, the garden a jungle of weeds and mud. Outside, a pair of trainers crept past, inches from her face as she lay holding her breath. They passed on by and she sighed with relief, then screamed as an eye peered back at her from a bloody face. She woke, heart pounding and bed-clothes in a knot, too afraid to examine the meaning of the dream.

Finally, the sun fought through muffling grey clouds, bringing the relief of a new day. In the shower, Gabrielle washed away the queasy tired feeling, then took her coffee into the garden and walked around looking at the plants and the fallen leaves. She remembered waking in the night, hearing a sound – of course, it was the galvanised bucket which stood by the tap. Maybe a hedgehog had bumped into it or caught a snail on it or whatever they do at night. That would explain the clanking sound she had heard in the night. She glanced towards the tap. The bucket was gone. Frowning, she walked round towards the counselling room door and stopped with a shock. The bucket had been placed upside down under the window of that room. Going closer she could see it was pressed deeply into the flower bed, bisecting a gerbera. She would never do such a thing. Someone had stood on the bucket to try to see into the room, or worse, might have tried to open the window while she slept. She shuddered. Leaving the gerbera to its fate – at least for the moment – she went inside to phone the police.

It was tempting to dial emergency services but reason prevailed. Instead she rattled through her bag till she found the card Carol, the policewoman, had given her. She explained the situation to the voice-mail and enunciated her phone number and address. Then she went back to the garden to pick the broken-stemmed flower which poked out from under the bucket. She put it in a glass on the kitchen window sill, pleased that its orange-red petals were still intact.

A police car pulled up and Carol got out.

Together they studied the bucket and the murdered gerbera.

The policewoman frowned. 'We don't take these things lightly. I'll get someone round to take fingerprints. What's inside there?'

Gabrielle explained that the bucket was under the window of her counselling room. The room had a door into the garden so that clients could enter without going through the house.

'There's nothing valuable in there, only a few ornaments and my files. I think any burglar would have seen it's not worth the effort. I do lock the filing cabinet and hide the key.'

'In the desk drawer?'

'Mmm. Well, I'll put it somewhere safer. After yesterday, I have to admit I'm a bit spooked.'

Carol was studying the window of the counselling room thoughtfully.

'It does seem a bit odd that we met yesterday at your client's flat and now your counselling room has been broken into. Any idea what they might have been after?'

'How do you mean?'

Carol didn't elaborate. 'It would be a great help if we could see your file on Jasmine Lawson. I could get a subpoena of course but if you would give it to me now it would save on paperwork.'

Gabrielle went inside and fetched the file. As she handed it over, she hoped that the torn-out page was not obvious.

When Carol drove away, Gabrielle picked up the phone. She needed her friend more than she needed caution.

'Kathy, hi. I could do with some fresh air. Are you free for a walk?'

They arranged to meet at the bridge in half an hour.

Since school days, the two women had been friends or 'co-conspirators' as Kathy called it. They had had their first cigarette together and shared their first taste of Kathy's father's gin. It was to Kathy that Gabrielle poured out her heart when she first realised she was attracted to girls. When her six year relationship broke up, she cried on Kathy's shoulder and let her friend tell her she was too good for Brenda anyway.

In her turn, Kathy had come to Gabrielle when she found she was pregnant and together they had agonised over the options. When Kathy and Jim got married Gabrielle feared she would lose her best-ever friend. Now they had three sons, two of them teenagers and the third a little younger, and while Kathy grumbled, it wasn't hard to see that she was proud of their 'boys will be boys' exploits. But in spite of the hubbub of family life, Kathy was still the most loyal of friends.

'What's up?' she asked as she locked the car and zipped up her jacket.

'Oh god, Kathy, there's been a murder and then I had a prowler last night.'

Kathy raised her eyebrows. 'Well, I'm glad you phoned. Let's walk while you tell me about it.'

They walked in silence for a while as Gabrielle gathered her thoughts. The path took them over the bridge and in a long curve by the river. Willows leaning over the water dropped their last few yellow leaves into the eddies. Little wax-eyes hopped from twig to twig cheeping incessantly like baby chicks. From a dogwood a tui gave its chuckling call followed by a cadenza of flute-like notes.

Gabrielle paused by a bend in the river which formed a deep pool. In the summer it was a great place for children to swim. Now it looked cold and foreboding.

Kathy paused too and was quiet for a moment. Her red curls lifted in the breeze and her hazel eyes darkened with worry.

'Gloomy, isn't it?' She shivered. 'So what's this about a murder? There was something on the radio this morning.'

'Can I talk to you in strictest confidence?' Gabrielle asked.

Her friend looked hurt. 'That's a bit formal isn't it? You know I don't blab your secrets.'

'The point is, it's not about me. You'd have to promise not to say a word, not even to Jim.'

Kathy nodded. 'I promise.'

'That murder. I think a client of mine might have done it. The police took away my notes on her, and, well, I think I'm being stalked.'

Gabrielle explained how she found Don's body, and about the bucket under the window.

'The police officer didn't say much but I have a feeling it's my client trying to get her notes because they are incriminating.'

Kathy looked even more concerned. 'Are you safe? You're there on your own such a lot.'

'I don't think she'd hurt me. Besides, we did that self-defence course, remember?'

'I don't see how that would help in a real attack.'

'Well, ok, I'm creeped out but what can I do? Just lock up carefully and refuse to act like a victim. It was probably a feeble attempt at burglary and there wasn't anything valuable to find so whoever it was knows not to come back.'

'Maybe. But if anything else happens promise me you'll phone the police right away. This town isn't all sweetness and light, you know. The Women's Centre is a great place for hearing what goes on and some of it's really dangerous. Don't take any risks, Gabe.'

'I'll be careful, I promise.'

'I'd better get back,' said Kathy, 'the boys will be home from school soon.'

'I feel much better, thanks for coming,' said Gabrielle.

'Well if you have the least worry you know you can always sleep over at our place.'

Gabrielle hugged her friend and drove home to tackle the paperwork. If she acted normally, perhaps all this weirdness would go away.

Chapter Three

In a small town it never takes long to connect the dots. The next day Gabrielle had a call from a nurse at the Mental Health Unit. They had admitted a young woman from the Emergency Department who named Gabrielle as her contact person. The girl was very withdrawn and was not saying much to the staff. Her name was Jasmine Lawson.

'How soon could you get down to see her?' asked the nurse.

Gabrielle checked her watch. Her first client was at nine-thirty, that meant she had about an hour. 'I'll come now,' she said.

The Unit had been built to replace the old Asylum on the outskirts of town and her counselling class had gone to the official blessing and opening about five years ago, but she had not been there since. Most of her clients were struggling with problems in their lives but so far none had been ill enough to need to be admitted to in-patient treatment.

She parked in front of the long low building in the grounds of the main hospital. The main door was open and she stepped into a foyer where a large painting filled the space with colour. The interior beyond was tasteful and tranquil. So tranquil in fact that no one seemed to notice her. Since the staff did not wear uniforms it was hard to know who to approach but the problem was solved by a woman approaching her.

'Are you looking for someone?'

She was a little heavily made up for so early in the day and was awaiting Gabrielle's answer with a bright red smile. As an afterthought she put out her hand.

'I'm Heidi.'

Gabrielle shook her hand, resisting the temptation to say: 'Heidi – hi!' She explained that she why she was there.

'Oh yes!' said Heidi. 'This way.'

Heidi led the way past a row of single rooms and stopped outside one. Gabrielle glanced at the name card and peered through the glass panel. The huddled form on the bed must be Jasmine. Heidi lifted her hand to knock but Gabrielle intervened.

'No, I don't want to wake her. Perhaps I could start by talking to someone. Do you know who it was who phoned me?'

Heidi marched back down the corridor and across a large lounge where people were gathering to sit in a circle of chairs. She veered off to the left and rapped on a door. Through the glass Gabrielle could see three or four people sitting at desks, talking on the phone or to each other. Heidi knocked again and a young man looked up, whereupon she pointed exaggeratedly to Gabrielle. He came over and opened the door.

'Visitor for Jasmine,' said Heidi.

'Thank you, Heidi. I'll handle this now. It's time for Group.'

Heidi gave him the finger, smiled sweetly at Gabrielle and stalked off.

'Oh, she's a .. er.. '

The nurse smiled. 'Client. Yes. Takes her duties as ward hostess very seriously though. How can I help?'

Gabrielle explained again. The nurse introduced himself as Barry and invited her into the office. He called to a young woman to join them and introduced her as Jasmine's doctor, Philippa Cole.

Doctors and policemen really are getting younger, thought Gabrielle. Philippa explained how Jasmine came to be in the Unit.

'It seems she spent the night with friends, partying hard. She passed out some time after midnight and the friends left her to sleep on the couch. In the morning her boyfriend came looking for her.'

'Boyfriend?' thought Gabrielle.

'He found her lying on the couch in a pool of blood and roused the flat with his shouts. They called the ambulance. She had cut both wrists with a pair of scissors.'

'Is she going to be all right?' asked Gabrielle.

'The cuts were stitched in the Emergency Department. She's not in any medical danger, but the registrar took note of how withdrawn and angry she seemed and was concerned she might do it again. She spent a night in hospital then yesterday she was transferred here.'

Barry added, 'She won't talk to anyone here, either. That's why we called you. You might be able to get through since you know her.'

Barry led Gabrielle back to Jasmine's room. He knocked, opened the door and said loudly, 'Someone to see you, Jasmine.'

He crossed the room and opened the curtains. The shape on the bed didn't move. Barry looked at her closely then nodded to Gabrielle.

'She's awake. I'll leave you to it.'

Gabrielle looked around. The room was simple, just a bed, a built-in dresser and a chair. The curtains and duvet cover were brightly coloured. The only sign of personal possessions was a small pair of trainers placed neatly beside the door.

The young woman on the bed was slightly built, dressed in jeans and a sweatshirt. A cotton blanket lay crumpled as if someone had tried to cover her up in the night but she had shoved it away.

Gabrielle picked up the chair from under the window and placed it where she could see the young woman's face, under her wing of blonde hair. Her eyes were open but unfocussed, her breathing almost imperceptible.

Gabrielle began speaking softly . She explained that the staff had called her because they were concerned about her.

'I was worried myself when you missed your appointment,' Gabrielle added. 'I went to your flat to see if you were all right.'

For the first time Jasmine showed some sign of hearing her. Her eyes flickered as she reached out and seized Gabrielle's hand. A bandage encircled her wrist like a sweat band. But still she said nothing.

Gabrielle leaned closer. 'Tell me what happened, Jasmine.'

Jasmine dropped Gabrielle's hand and turned away so that her hair covered her face. Her lips moved soundlessly.

'Jasmine, talk to me. I can help,' urged Gabrielle.

Though she doubted the truth of that. It might not be right to ask the young woman to incriminate herself. And if Jasmine didn't know that her father was dead, was this the time to tell her? She sat for a while in silence, debating what to do next.

Slowly, Jasmine's eyes closed as if to shut her out. Gabrielle rose, placed her card on the dresser and went back to the nurses' office to find Barry. She saw him exhorting the circle of clients in the lounge so she spoke to the young doctor.

'I don't think Jasmine's ready to talk. I'll come back in a day or two, shall I?'

Philippa nodded. 'We'll keep her under close observation, she's still a high suicide risk. I've started her on an anti-depressant but that will take a while to kick in. She'll be here a while yet so it would be good if you could keep in touch.'

Gabrielle assured Philippa she would do that. She was about to leave when a middle-aged woman with improbably flaxen hair and very blue eye shadow came in and addressed the doctor abruptly.

'I'm Jasmine Lawson's mother,' she said, 'here are some clothes for her.' She handed over a supermarket bag and turned to go.

Gabrielle intercepted her with a smile.

'I'm Gabrielle Murphy, Jasmine's counsellor. I'm so glad to meet you.' She held out her hand.

The woman looked her up and down, ignoring the outstretched hand. Her skin had the sallow, lined look of a chain smoker but the dyed hair and the make-up said 'I'm pretty dammit!'

She said harshly, 'Don't you look so smug; this is all your fault with your touchy-feely feminist ideas. Some things are family business and should be kept that way.'

She shouldered past Gabrielle and went out the door.

******

Jasmine lay on the bed with her knees drawn up. She made herself small, like a child sent to bed after a beating, camouflaged by stillness. She watched the curtains billowing softly as if they were breathing gently in time to her own breath. In, out, one, in, out, two. If she counted the breaths she could make her mind blank. In, out... When she was a child she had taken herself away in her mind. She could look at the parrots on her wallpaper and she would be a missionary in Africa, bringing the Bible to people whose skin was as black as her Labrador, Dusky. They would turn their kind faces towards her just as he did and she would stand under trees heavy with huge bright flowers and tell them that God loved them too, just as he loved her and Dusky. A sharp pain in her belly reminded her that Dusky had gone: Dad gave him to the SPCA the night before... before... The flowers, the parrots, the kind dark faces, vanished like a popped bubble. She counted her breaths: in, out, ten, in, out, eleven...

Susi was knocking on the door, calling from the hallway.

'You have to come to dinner, Mum says right this minute.'

Jasmine thought of cold gravy and congealed mashed spuds and her stomach contracted. The door opened. It wasn't Susi, it was Heidi, bustling in with all the self-importance of any older sister.

'Jasmine? You have to eat. Come on, it's macaroni cheese.'

Jasmine kept counting till Heidi went away. She tried to picture herself as a small child in those happy times when Susi would let her tag along on 'big kids' adventures'. Mostly that meant raiding Mrs Doris's fruit trees. Susi would send Jasmine up to the high branches where the ripest fruit hung temptingly, and because she was so small the thin twigs held her weight. Bare feet curling round the rough bark, she would reach out for the soft, warm plums and throw them down to Susi. Unfortunately her big sister was not a good catch and a lot of the plums went splat on the ground. It made Jasmine's head spin to see Susi so small down there on the grass but she would never admit fear in case Susi said she was too babyish to play with.

Sometimes Mrs Doris came out and shooed them away but she was nowhere near as scary as Mum. Once Jasmine, sick of getting all the splatted plums that Susi left her, filled the pockets of her shorts with some of the best. But the plums squashed anyway when she climbed down and she got a hiding from Mum for staining her shorts.

Then there was the time when Susi took her down to the back of the section where a matted honeysuckle vine made a magic cave. Jasmine would have been happy to sit there sucking honey from the base of the flowers, but Susi had pinched one of Mum's cigarettes and some matches. One puff made Jasmine cough and wheeze and she would not try again, but Susi pretended she liked it and kept going until she was green and retching. They crawled out leaving the butt smouldering and later that afternoon the honeysuckle was ablaze. Mum ran down with the garden hose and swore at the neighbours for lighting their inciner-ator so close to the boundary, so no one ever blamed the kids. The loss of the cave was punishment enough to Jasmine.

She never did take up smoking but right now she longed for some of Davey's P. The stuff they gave you here in the Unit did nothing at all but P – aah, that took all your worries away.

Chapter Four

During the day, it occurred to Gabrielle that one of the people who would hold a major piece of the puzzle was her brother. As the pathologist at the local hospital Toby would be responsible for examining any unexplained bodies. He worked hard but surely, family man that he was, he would be at home on a Thursday evening.

Toby opened the door in track pants, T-shirt and bare feet. It was hard to see him as the distinguished medical specialist and expert witness of his working life. His brown hair was beginning to recede and Gabrielle thought she could see grey threads on his temples, though he was not yet thirty-five.

'Gabe! Good to see you, sis. Come in.'

She hesitated. 'It's work-related, Toby, I hope you don't mind. I need to talk something over with you.'

'We can talk in the lounge. Crystal is just putting Zoe to bed.' He stood aside and she stepped past him into the hall, dodging the toys on the floor and the push-chair which leaned against the wall.

'What is it, honey?' Crystal appeared in the doorway with Zoe on her hip. The light from the dining-room made the little girl's baby-white curls look like a dandelion clock. Crystal appeared to be wearing a checked shirt of Toby's over faded jeans but even so her dancer's body looked lithe and slim and her short black hair shone. Gabrielle kissed her cheek, then kissed the baby.

'How's my favourite niece?'

'I'm just about to pop her down. Want a cuddle? Look Zoe, it's Aunty Gabrielle.'

Gabrielle held out her arms and the little girl leaned forward. She moulded herself into her aunt's body and Gabrielle nuzzled the soft hair, enjoying the biscuity smell of her.

'We've got some work stuff to talk about, we'll be in the lounge for a while,' said Toby.

Zoe held her arms out to her Dad who took her, kissed her and ruffled her curls, then passed her back to her mother.

He turned to his sister.

'Come and have a seat. What's it about?'

Gabrielle followed him into the lounge that was bright and neat with Crystal's touch – so different from visiting her little brother in his foul med-school flats. She still hadn't quite got used to him as a family man with a wife, a child, a mortgage and a consultant's position. She sat on a lime-green chair and put a blue cushion on her lap.

'I don't know how much you can tell me,' she said. 'I need to know how someone died.'

'Gabrielle, you know I can't say anything. My pathology work's confidential.'

'I know, but Toby I'm really worried that a client of mine might have killed someone.'

Toby stiffened. Gabrielle could see that he knew at once who she meant. No doubt Don's body was in his morgue as they spoke.

'Could it have been an accident, like someone pushed him and he fell and hit his head? Or was a knife or some weapon involved?'

'All I can tell you is it definitely wasn't an accident. You must know that, they said on the radio that it was a homicide investigation.'

'Do you think a young girl could have done it on her own?'

'Look, I'm sorry, Sis, but we really can't talk about it. If what you're saying is true we could both end up in court on this case. Gabe, leave this to the police, it's their job and if your client's innocent she'll be fine.'

He looked at her a moment, then said, 'Hang on, I might have something.' He left the room and came back with a leaflet.

'Your client might need a good defence. I was at a conference where this woman was a guest speaker, very interesting. She's a forensic psychologist and did her thesis on women who kill. I was pretty impressed with what she had to say.' Toby grinned. 'Plus she looked as if she might play for your team.'

Gabrielle frowned at him. 'You can say the L word you know.'

'Does "dyke" begin with L?' he asked mock-innocent.

Gabrielle whacked him on the arm, then took the leaflet and gave him a hug.

'Thanks, little bro.'

Toby looked seriously at her. 'It's nasty stuff, Gabes, don't get mixed up in it. Just do your job and leave the investigation to the professionals.'

'Of course, ' said Gabrielle, ' why would you think otherwise?'

'Well, you always did want to be a cop, didn't you?'

'Dad squashed that, he had some pretty Victorian ideas about what work was suitable for a lady.'

'No, I think he knew you would be soft as butter. Look at you now, bleeding heart that you are.'

He ducked as she took another swing at him and grinned.

'Never could fight either.'

'That was Mum's fault, she always broke us up before it got interesting.'

They said in unison, '"I'll separate you children."'

'Like an egg, I imagined, it sounded dangerous!' added Gabrielle.

Toby flung an arm around her shoulders.

'Anyway, try calling that woman tomorrow. Now, I can't offer you dinner, we eat early and I was starving so there aren't even any leftovers, but come and have a coffee with us. Crystal will have the kettle on if Zoe's gone off to sleep.'

Gabrielle glanced at the leaflet and put it safely in her pocket as she went through to the kitchen.

'By the way,' she said, 'I'm going to see Aunt Lil tomorrow. Want to come?'

Toby grinned at her ruefully. 'I think you're much better at that than I am. Besides, I'll be at work all day.'

Gabrielle shook her head at him. 'You should make the effort. She won't be around much longer.'

After coffee Gabrielle drove home thinking how great it was to have a brother. On the farm they had egged each other on to climb the highest tree, ride their ponies faster, swim across the creek or brave the bull in his paddock. They had squabbled, of course, and Gabrielle had teased her little brother mercilessly until he got big enough and smart enough to retaliate, but they were instantly united against any outside threat. If he was warning her off getting involved in Jasmine's case, he was no doubt feeling protective of her.

As she thought about his life now she felt a familiar twinge. One of the worst aspects of realising that she was gay had been the knowledge that she may never have children. Sure, lesbians did, one way or another, but there was no guarantee it would be possible for her and as she was already well into her thirties, without a partner, time was running out. That felt deeply sad.

Chapter Five

'I need a ramp or a hand saw.'

Aunt Lil peered around the room and searched the baggy pockets of her cardigan. She sniffed pointedly and rolled the fabric of her floral skirt between finger and thumb.

'A hanky?' suggested Gabrielle.

Lil nodded as if her niece was slow on the uptake.

Gabrielle found a handkerchief in the top drawer of the dresser and tucked it into Lil's pocket. She would have liked to brush her wild grey hair but she didn't want to patronise the old lady.

She took her aunt's arm. 'Come on, Lil. We're going out for coffee.' Glancing down to check that Lil had shoes on her feet, Gabriel grimaced at the sight of purple socks and bare shins. Maybe socks were easier for the staff to manage than pantyhose but they looked odd.

Aunt Lil began peering and pocket-searching again. She found the hanky and shook her head at it. Gabrielle caught it as it fluttered to the floor.

Her aunt's voice shook a little. 'I haven't got any flumpert. You know, to pay.'

'You don't need to worry about that.'

Lil allowed herself to be led from the room as she muttered about being a burden.

Gabrielle signed the book and told the nurse, who looked like a schoolgirl, that they would be back in an hour.

The cafe was a short drive away and the owner knew Lil and Gabrielle from their weekly visits.

'Two flat whites and a muffin to share?' she asked.

Gabrielle thanked her and helped Lil to a chair as the espresso machine began to snort. The salt and pepper shakers on the table were a china man and woman. Lil picked up the china woman and turned her upside down.

'No privates,' she said loudly.

It was amazing how clearly the words came out when it was something embarrassing. Gabrielle took the salt shaker and put it back by the vase of silk hydrangeas. She brushed salt off the table and, reaching into her bag, pulled out a magazine.

'Look, I brought you a Woman's Weekly. Let's see what news they've got.'

They looked at the pictures and Gabrielle summarised the captions. Lil could still make a good stab at the headlines. She read slowly, 'Royal baby in hotel emergency.'

There was no point correcting that to 'hospital'. Gabrielle was well aware how easily they could get bogged down and Lil could be quite sharp if she thought her niece was being obtuse.

The coffee arrived and two plates, each with half a muffin and a dollop of cream topped with a strawberry.

Lil's hand hovered over the coffee, then the muffin. She pulled the cup and saucer dangerously close to the edge of the table and dug into the froth with the cake fork.

'Like this.' Gabrielle picked up her cup and sipped.

'Why would I drink out of your cup?' snapped Lil. But she put down the fork and lifted her cup with both hands.

Gabrielle sighed. A year ago she used to visit Aunt Lil in her own home. Lil would make the coffee and they talked about politics and literature. It was Lil who had developed Gabrielle's taste for classical music by lending her CDs and taking her to concerts. For some months neither of them could believe that the older woman's formidable brain was failing her. But eventually it became too obvious to avoid.

Twice Gabrielle arrived to find the smoke alarm screeching and Lil on a chair trying to swat it with a tea towel. She asked Gabrielle to take the battery out. 'It's faulty, it keeps going off.'

Instead Gabrielle turned off the oven and used the tea towel to carry a charred lump in tinfoil out on to the back lawn. Back inside, she questioned her aunt. 'I thought you had Meals on Wheels. Why are you cooking?'

Lil was defiant. 'The meal arrives lukewarm, I was heating it up.'

The third mishap was more serious. Gabrielle arrived one morning to find Lil sitting on the back steps, her face and hands blue and chilled. She had locked herself out the previous night while fetching kindling.

'But Lil I thought we'd agreed that you wouldn't light the fire. You have that new electric heater, remember?'

Lil had spent the night in the woodshed on a pile of sacks. Cold and confused by the time Gabrielle found her, she had a rambling tale of how a Chinese family had commandeered the house and laughed at her when she knocked and called. Lil, who had never been racist, was hurt about this.

Gabrielle got the spare key from the shed and let them in. She called an ambulance, then turned off the TV which was blaring out a cartoon show with canned laughter. She put Lil's coat around her shoulders and a rug over her knees and made her a strong cup of tea while they waited for the paramedics.

Lil was in hospital for three days that time and Gabrielle had called her cousin in Auckland. She told him it was time to come down and make some decisions about his mother. They found the Willowbank Rest Home and although Lil protested that you couldn't have a decent conversation with anyone in the place, she was safe and well-cared for there.

Lil drained her coffee cup and tackled the muffin with her teaspoon. She managed it neatly, ate the strawberry, leaf and all, and pushed the plate away. Gabrielle got up to pay.

'I haven't finished yet.'

She took a spoonful of whipped cream, teetered it across the table and opened her mouth wide. The cream fell in her lap. She scooped it up surprisingly deftly and popped it into her mouth. Gabrielle pushed the plate closer, thought 'I can't look' and went to the counter.

Lil cleaned up the cream on her plate and reached for Gabrielle's.

'Let's go. You can take the Woman's Weekly if you like.'

The diversion worked and they made their way back to the car.

Gabrielle took Lil back to the rest home. As she left, she tried not to look back at the bewildered face which peered after her through the locked glass door. She suppressed a pang of guilt and hurried home to wrap up her paperwork for the day.

* * * * * *

Gabrielle was about to go and make herself a meal, when there was a tap at the counselling room door. She opened it to a tattooed Maori man who was built like an All Black. On his forehead the blue-black arches of his moko were furrowed with worry.

'Hi Gabe, I saw the light was on. Is this ok?'

'Garth! Come in.'

She stood aside to let him in and waved him towards a chair. He sat with his hands clasped between his knees.

'Cuppa?'

He shook his head.

'What's up?'

'It's our boarder. He's vamoosed.'

'I didn't know you had a boarder,' said Gabrielle.

'Talia had this idea to get us out of debt. Actually, I think it was your mate's idea.'

'Kathy?'

'Yeah, Kathy. We went to the English school and got this little Nepali fella, he's going to study forestry when his English is better. Nice guy, helluva sense of humour and very patient with our kid. Cooks a mean curry too. He was part of the whanau right away. Last night he didn't come home. Talia was worried but I said chill, girl, maybe he got lucky. But this afternoon the school phoned, he didn't turn up today. When I got home from work Talia sent me round to talk to you.'

'Shouldn't you call the police?'

Garth sighed. 'That's the problem. Seems the cops came to the school yesterday, wanted to talk to Ram – that's his name, Ramchandra . Didn't say what about. He hasn't been seen since.'

'Did you check his room?'

'We did. He must have come in while Talia was at playgroup with Ruben. His backpack, sleeping bag and boots are gone, and his jacket too, but he would have worn that to school, it was cold yesterday. And Talia says there's stuff missing from the pantry, muesli and biscuits and teabags. Reckon he's gone bush.'

'Surely the police will go after him.'

'He doesn't have much trust in the police, he says they're pretty dodgy in his part of the world. Anyway, if he's done something stupid, like take a joyride in someone's car or something, we'd want to stand by him, try to work it out. We don't want him sent home.'

Gabrielle waited. Garth clearly had a plan worked out.

He hesitated. 'I could go up there tomorrow but it would be better if you came too. He might need some persuading.'

Gabrielle thought for a moment. Safety first.

'Is he ok for another night in the bush? It's going to be cold again.'

'He's sussed. He used to take tourists into the mountains back home. He's tough for such a little guy.'

'Where would he go?'

'Well, me and some of the boys took him pig-hunting up the Pelorus. He knows there are huts up there and that it's a bit out of the way.'

'What's the Pelorus like?'

'No tourists, which is good for keeping a low profile. But a bit rough. You wouldn't want to get off the track. A bloke fell down a bluff and broke his leg last month. It was three days before they found him, he was lucky to make it. But the huts are good, there's bunks with mattresses and plenty of firewood and water.'

'Is he armed?' She was not at all keen to play Rambo in the bush with an armed Asian she didn't know.

'He has this bloody great knife, a khukri he calls it. Uses it for every-thing from splitting kindling to cutting his toenails. He'll have that with him. But he's cool. I don't think he'd hurt anyone – he's Buddhist or something, like a Rasta.'

She wanted to agree to go with him. For one thing, she was a keen tramper and she had not been out in the bush for a while. For another, she wanted to shake off the recurring image of the murdered man, and a stiff walk in the hills usually proved most effective when she needed to clear her head. Besides, Garth had offered to take her tramping once before but then he had reneged.

'Talia isn't happy about me going bush with another woman,' he had said, 'You know Talia, she thinks every chick in town is going to jump my bones. I'd tell her it's not true but I like her to think she's got a good catch here. So I thought how about you bring Kathy? What's that saying about two birds in the bush?'

'I think what Talia is after is the one about three's a crowd,' Gabrielle had said with a wry smile. She had suggested it to Kathy who had laughed, saying that going tramping with Gabrielle would be bad enough but the pace Garth would set ... So she hadn't gone into the hills with him after all.

Gabrielle was happy to have another opportunity. She liked Garth and she respected his knowledge of the bush. A day out with him would be a challenge and a chance to learn.

'So you'll pick me up about eight then?'

Garth grinned, the tattooed spirals on his cheeks folding into waves. 'Choice. Is that cuppa still on offer? Talia sent me straight round without my dinner. She's mad at me for not doing something about this last night.'

Gabrielle nodded. He followed her into the kitchen and while she put the kettle on he sat at the table. The spindle-backed chair gave a little gasp but it held his weight.

'How's Ruben? I saw him in town with Talia last week, he's growing fast.'

'He's cool. He's Daddy's boy. Talia's jealous she can't get near him when I'm home. He'll be two next month – all the whanau are coming down for a big do. You'll come, eh?'

'I'd love to.'

They made an unlikely pair. Garth, a big Maori man in his late twenties with shaven head and traditional tattoos on his forehead and cheeks, could command respect or even fear when needed. Even though Gabrielle was in her thirties she still looked like the farmer's daughter that she was. Her blue eyes lacked guile and often her brown hair was caught up in a pony-tail as if she was sixteen. When she was dressed in jeans and a T-shirt without make-up it was only the smile lines in the corners of her eyes that showed her age. A year ago Kathy's husband Jim had introduced Gabrielle to Garth at a barbecue. She was used to meeting Jim's forestry mates but she was a bit taken aback to be introduced to Garth, especially when Jim told her with a smirk that Garth was not long out of prison. Feeling that Jim had unfairly put both of them on the spot, she had made a point of showing an interest in prison life just as if she was entertaining one of her mother's bridge club friends. She had asked about the moko too, learning that it was a traditional design which belonged to his family and as the eldest son he had the right to wear it.

For his part, one of Garth's more positive experiences inside had been his sessions with the prison psychologist and where Jim's mates usually made shrink jokes to hide their unease, he respected Gabrielle's work as a counsellor. They got on so well that Talia had loomed up to introduce herself and baby Ruben in a clear 'hands off he's mine' message. Over time, Gabrielle had become a friend of the family and she tried to let Talia know she had no intention of stealing her man. That hadn't succeeded entirely, but Gabrielle hesitated to come right out with the news that she was gay. She had no idea how the family would take it .

Garth finished his tea and biscuits and got up to go. He took Gabrielle's hand gently and kissed her cheek, in the Maori way. As she closed and locked the door behind him, she looked up at the dark hills with clear frosty stars above them. The Nepali man would need to have a good fire going.

Chapter Six

It was late on Friday evening when Gabrielle went back into her counselling room and looked at the leaflet Toby had given her. Martina Day,
Forensic Psychologist. There was a thumbnail sketch of her career.

'Martina Day lectures in criminology at the University of Victoria,
Wellington and has specialised in forensic profiling, that is, matching
the type of person to the crime. Age, gender, size and strength all
affect the method chosen, as do the level of intelligence, ability to
plan and think ahead, motivation. Dr Day's Ph D thesis was on women
who kill. She also has an interest in issues surrounding domestic
violence.'

Gabrielle remembered the name. Martina had been interviewed on
TV at the time of the Wellington serial rapist and had given a profile
of the type of person who would do this. When they caught him she had
proved to have been close to the mark.

Forensic psychology sounded interesting. It was not usually relevant
to the counselling work that Gabrielle did, but she was a keen reader of
detective fiction and one of her favourite TV programmes had a feisty
woman profiler who often saved the day.

There was a Wellington contact number on the leaflet and, doubting
that anyone would be there, she thought she could just leave a message.
She was surprised to hear a low voice answer, 'Martina speaking.'

Gabrielle took the plunge and explained what had happened and
how the police had taken Jasmine's file and how concerned she felt about

Jasmine. It was a relief to talk about it and Martina seemed a good listener, interested in the story.

'I'll be in Nelson next week for another workshop, why don't we meet then?'

Gabrielle hesitated. 'Um, your fee?'

Martina laughed. 'No fee. Let's just meet for coffee and you can tell me more.'

'Oh, well thank you that would be great, just say where.'

'I'll be staying at the Rutherford, there's a café there I believe. After the workshop on Monday, say 5.30.'

Gabriell put the phone down with a sense of relief. There would be someone to share the burden with, and quite soon.

* * * * * *

The dog had a gaunt, eager look as it pushed on up the track. Gabrielle felt her breath rasp in her throat but she trudged on, not keen to call another halt so soon. Up ahead she could see Garth moving quickly and quietly through the trees. He was surprisingly agile for such a big man. She fixed her eyes on his backpack where an orange tag swung back and forth with each step, and she focussed on pulling in each breath with her diaphragm. Wet leaves flicked her face and her boots made squishing noises.

The fine mist which deprived them of the view of snow-covered mountains soon soaked them. Gabrielle consoled herself by picturing the hot bath that she would have when she got home.

Garth called back in a stage whisper, 'Hut's just here. Stay quiet. I don't want him to run.'

They set off again, one foot after the other. Soon Gabrielle could see the angle of the hut roof on the skyline, its straight edge incongruous in the bush. Relief gave her a surge of strength and she caught up with Garth who was moving through the trees as stealthily as one of his ancestors staging an ambush.

The hut stood in a grassy clearing on the other side of a small stream. There was no smoke from the chimney but perhaps Ram had doused the fire in preparation for leaving.

The dog watched Garth's face.

Garth whispered, ' We'll cross further down, then you go round the back. I'll go in first. If he's there he'll have his knife. '

They backed up until they were out of sight of the hut and found a way across the stream. It was snow fed. Gabrielle thought sadly of her cosy socks, then stepped into the water, suppressing a gasp as she trudged across on the submerged rocks. Icy water swirled around her ankles and when she stepped on to the bank it flowed from her boots in runnels.

On the other bank they separated and Garth went up to the hut door. He opened it slowly, saying, 'Ram, Ram are you there, mate?'

Then he waved to her to come. The hut was empty. Not only empty of the Nepali man but of any trace he had been there. The ashes in the fireplace were cold and gave nothing away. The benches were clear and clean, with no note, no sign.

They looked at each other. Gabrielle felt annoyed at the wasted effort.

Garth went outside and put two fingers in his mouth, giving a piercing whistle.

Kuri looked eagerly up at him. He whistled again and studied the bush and the mist. Kuri ran a little way and yelped.

'Reckon she's got a scent.' He looked at the sky. 'We've got about six hours' daylight. Better get cracking.'

They took up their packs and Garth clicked his fingers at Kuri. She scrambled to her feet.

'Where is he, girl? Show us now.'

She gave a little bark and set off into the undergrowth.

Garth raised his eyebrows at Gabrielle. 'She doesn't bother with tracks. Can you manage a bit of bush-bashing?'

Gabrielle, sensing a challenge, grinned back. 'Of course.'

They said little more for the next hour as they scrambled over rocks and ducked under branches and vines. Once Garth had to come back to disentangle Gabrielle from the hooks of a bush lawyer vine, and once she tripped on a root and fell heavily to the ground. She picked herself up, glad he hadn't seen.

Suddenly they were almost on top of Kuri who had stopped in front of a large fern. She gave a soft yip as Garth put his hand on her collar.

'Look, the fern's broken here,' he said, 'go easy now.'

Crouching down he lifted the heavy fronds. Crumbling soil gave way in skid marks which ended abruptly. Leaning forward cautiously, Garth peered through the fern.

He rocked back on his heels and looked at Gabrielle. 'Quite a drop, you can't see it for the fern. Maybe Ram fell.' He leaned forward and called, 'Hullo! You there mate?'

They both strained to listen. Amid the sound of the stream below came a faint cry.

'Ok,' said Garth, 'let's try this.'

He began to lower himself over a boulder and search for holds in the cliff. Gabrielle watched as he disappeared below the edge. She knelt on the rock and peered over. Garth was straddled against the cliff, clutching a straggly bush in one hand. It didn't look strong enough to hold his weight. He inched down.

Among the bushes there was a fluttering, something red. Gabrielle called out and pointed to it.

Garth looked up. Sweat beaded his face and made the lines of his moko gleam.

'Yes!' said Garth. There was a shape in the bushes, halfway down the rock-face, where a cloth fluttered from a branch. Gabrielle cooled her scraped hands on a patch of moss and watched as Garth reached the little flag.

He called up, 'It's him ok. Come down.'

Gabrielle set off as she had seen Garth do, choosing each hold carefully. One hand, one foot, then the other, and the other. She didn't look down and thought only about the next hold. Suddenly Garth's voice was right beside her head.

'Good stuff. Just over here a bit, there's a ledge.'

She got herself wedged onto a narrow rock ledge and looked at Ram. He was an ill-looking yellow colour and the lower part of his left leg lay at an awkward angle. He acknowledged her with a faint nod – he was conscious. Garth already had the water bottle at his lips. Gabrielle, remembering her first aid course, checked the Nepali man's pulse. It was feeble and erratic. His forehead was cold and clammy where pain had made him sweat. She ran her hands gently over his body: no damage till she came to the leg which she avoided touching. It was clearly broken and would hurt him terribly if he was moved.

She looked at Garth. 'We need the rescue helicopter.' She pulled out her cell phone, tried it, then shook her head. 'No signal from here.'

'I could carry him if we can get him up to the top.'

'His leg's broken. He's in pain already but it will be terrible if we move him.'

Garth looked at the sky. 'It will be dark in a few hours. If we don't make a move soon we'll be spending the night here.'

Ram whispered, 'Please carry me. I too long here.'

Gabrielle looked at him thoughtfully. 'It will hurt a lot. I can try to splint your leg but I have nothing to make it firm and only some mild pain-killers.'

He nodded. 'Do it.'

Gabrielle pulled off her pack and found the small first aid kit she carried. She gave Ram four of the pain-killers which she knew were too mild to be much help since they were mere headache pills, but he took them gratefully.

'Let them work for a bit. What can we do to pass a bit of time?'

Looking solemnly at Ram's pale face, Garth began to croon in Maori. The syllables flowed like water over pebbles and a tune took shape as Garth sang in a deep, rich, soothing voice. Gabrielle knew the tune but not the words so she hummed along, repeating the chorus. Ram, his eyes still closed, gave a little smile.

'Ka ru, ka ru, ka te i au e.'

When Garth stopped Gabrielle looked at him enquiringly.

'"Though we are happy there is much to fear and we must endure the stress of life to come out on top."'

Gabrielle smiled. 'Appropriate. Ok next stage.'

She pulled out a crepe bandage and looked around for something firm to tie to Ram's leg. He made a gesture to his pack which lay half under him. 'Khukri.'

Garth found the knife and cut a small branch.

'Hold him.' Gabrielle gritted her teeth as she pulled the leg straight. Ram screamed. Garth held his shoulders in a wrestler's grip and murmured to him. Trying not to think about the pain she was causing, she bound the leg to the branch, then unknotting the red bandana which had alerted them to where Ram lay, she tied his ankles together. It looked tragically inadequate but was all they could do.

'Now what?'

Garth looked up. 'Can you pick up his legs? I'll lift him from here.' He demonstrated by putting his arms around the Nepali man's trunk.

They positioned themselves, counted 'one, two, three' and lifted Ram till Garth could lay him on the ledge above them. The young man groaned and bit his lip. Sweat broke out on his face but he didn't scream again.

'Well done mate.' Ram now had his eyes tightly closed.

Gabrielle put the packet of pain-killers in her pocket and fastened her pack. She stretched up to grasp a boulder with both hands and was glad when Garth gave her a pull up to where she could stand a little to one side of Ram's feet. Garth looked further up.

'There's the top,' he said. 'We'll have to lift him up and over.'

Again they lifted Ram, Garth taking most of the weight and Gabrielle trying to keep his legs level so that there was as little movement on the broken bone as possible. They scrambled up through the ferns and laid Ram gently on soft fronds.

Gabrielle pulled out the cellphone. 'Damn, still no signal.'

'Climb a tree,' suggested Garth.

They looked around. Most of the bigger trees had smooth straight trunks, but a knotted beech tree looked possible. Gabrielle put her foot into Garth's clasped hands and let him boost her up to the first branches. When she climbed up into the canopy of the tree, the phone worked and she punched in the number. After explaining where they were, she asked for the rescue helicopter, then climbed down, ducking the twigs that scratched at her face.

She told Garth, 'They'll be half an hour. I said we'll be somewhere in the vicinity of the hut.'

'If I take him in a fireman's lift, we can make it.'

She helped Garth lift Ram over his shoulder and made sure he gripped the tightly bound legs well above the break.

'Lighter than a pig, that's for sure,' he said.

'I think he's passed out,' said Gabrielle, checking the pale face which hung down Garth's back.

They trudged through the bushes, retracing their steps.

'Shit,' said Garth, 'excuse me, but we forgot the dog.'

Gabrielle put two fingers in her mouth and gave a loud whistle.

'Where'd you learn that?' Garth was impressed.

'Dad's a sheep farmer remember. I know some great swear words too.' She whistled again.

They kept on at a steady pace. Gabrielle kept an eye on her watch and after about twenty minutes said, 'I think I should run ahead. They won't find us in this dense bush.'

Garth grunted and pointed with his chin. He had spotted the orange triangle that marked the track. 'Follow those,' he said.

She nodded and set off at a jog. The ground was level but tree roots and hollows could twist ankles and cause falls. She wiped sweat out of her eyes and concentrated on finding each marker.

When she heard the beating of the helicopter's rotors overhead, she broke into a run, pulling off her red jacket to wave above her. With relief she burst out into the open not far from the hut. She looked up and waved her jacket in big circles as the helicopter loomed out of the darkening sky.

She crouched and watched as it bent the ferns and scrubby bushes with a blast of air, before settling in the clearing near the hut. Two men in red overalls jumped out and she ran up to them, pointing back the way she had come.

They followed her with a stretcher. Garth, plodding along steadily with Ram on his shoulder, was not too far away and with relief he lowered his burden on to the stretcher. Ram stirred and groaned with the pain of the movement but did not regain consciousness and they hurried to get him settled into the back of the helicopter where the paramedics could work on him.

Garth said, 'I'll wait for Kuri.'

Gabrielle was only too pleased to ride back in the helicopter. As the pilot took off, she thought she could see a tiny shape emerge from the bushes and run up to Garth.

* * * * * *

'Police come, too many questions. I run away, stay in hut where you took me hunting.'

It was late on Sunday afternoon. Ram was propped up in his hospital bed with a cage over his plastered leg, telling his story to Garth and Gabrielle.

'I cook, make fire, sing Nepali songs. All alone in mountains make me sad for home. Then three men, four big dogs come. Laughing, beer drinking. They cook huge dinner, meat, vegetable, everything. Give me beer, meat. Very happy. Sleep that night not so good, men noisy, 'he made a snoring sound. 'In morning, I very tired, glad they go. They say hunting pig. Ok, good luck, I say. They ask what I do. I pretend not understand, smile, bye-bye.

Next night again men come back. Big pig dead, man carry on back like backpack. Blood smell, flies. They surprise to see me. Not so happy this time. Talk, talk quietly together. I worry. Think they tell police. Early morning I get up, take all things, think I sleep next night in bushes, find better place later. Then I hear men come, dogs. I afraid, they have guns. Maybe catch me, take to police for money. I run, then fall, bang. Wake up stuck on rock, leg hurting. I think I die there, Amma, my mother, never know what happened.'

There were tears in his eyes. 'I hear shouting, "Ram, Ram" ok must be friend. I shout back but too tired to make loud shout. I think maybe you go away. Then Garth jump over rock like monkey!' He grinned at the memory. 'You come like Hanuman, Monkey god, to save me.'

There was more to ask but he was too tired and sick to be questioned. They left him with chocolate and fruit and some of Talia's baking.

Chapter Seven

When Gabrielle pulled up outside the Rutherford on Monday evening she realised she had very little idea who she was meeting. She tried to recall the TV item about the serial killer but no face came to mind for Martina Day. Once in the café however, it wasn't difficult to pick her out. Around the bar, talking all at once, were half a dozen young people in his and hers lawyer uniforms. Seated by a window, a smart blonde with a very short skirt was turned attentively towards an older man. At the counter a slim woman in her thirties was ordering coffee. She had short spiky black hair and olive skin and was dressed in a charcoal grey suit with a bright blue collarless shirt.

Gabrielle went up to the counter. 'Martina? I'm Gabrielle Murphy.'

The woman smiled and held out her hand. Gabrielle shook it. It felt warm and firm.

'Can I get you a coffee?'

'A latte, thank you.' Gabrielle reached for her handbag but Martina said to the waitress, 'Put it on my tab,' and led the way to a table.

'How was the workshop?' asked Gabrielle.

'It's going well. Some of those young lawyers were there and they offered me a drink, so I guess that's a good sign. The police are always a bit sceptical about shrinks and boffins, but they're keen to learn and seem to have decided I know my stuff.'

'How do you win them over?'

Martina smiled. 'I appeal to their sense of logic and show them how to break a situation down.' She looked at Gabrielle to gauge her interest and, encouraged, continued. 'If you think of us as primates, and we're the most violent of them, then I ask what motivates primates?'

Gabrielle thought of nature programmes she had watched. 'Food and sex, I expect.'

'Close. Food and territory can be lumped together as survival. Sex definitely. But status is a major pre-occupation with all primates. There's continual jostling, testing one's strength, defending one's position. Status is a huge motivation for humans. It's just not PC to admit it.'

'I expect status makes sense to police.'

'Indeed. So then I apply the idea to murder – some murders are committed to assert status and punish a transgressor. Think of drug-related murders where a henchman is disposed of for getting out of line, or a customer for not paying. The boss asserts his authority. Often a cascade of events follows through paranoia and cover-ups but the basic point is to make it clear who's on top.'

'Isn't that a male thing, being top of the heap? I wouldn't think it applied so much to women.'

'Women are more likely to kill for survival: to protect themselves or their children. There's a big debate about whether a woman who has endured years of violence can claim to have killed in self-defence if she eventually retaliates. Usually women are smaller and not as strong as the man that beats them, they resort to using weapons or taking advantage of him when he's asleep, even drugging him or tying him up when he's drunk, to reverse the roles. That is, of course, pre-meditated and occurs when the violence has abated, so it doesn't fit the usual definition of self-defence, which is more about the heat of the moment.'

Martina paused and smiled. 'I'm lecturing you. Sorry. Once I get into my stride I might go for the full fifty minutes.'

Gabrielle laughed. 'That's fine, it's interesting. I can see you're keen on your subject.'

'So, tell me about your young woman.'

'She's 17, classic symptoms of childhood neglect – over-responsible, with social phobia, anhedonia...'

Martina made a 'stop' gesture. 'Never mind the diagnoses, we'll take them as read. What's she really like?'

Gabrielle blushed. Snapped! Trying to out-psych the psychologist.

'Small, wiry, a survivor. She's had to pretty much bring herself up and at the same time look after her mother who's an alcoholic. Since her overdose, she's been living alone in a flat, which is quite an achievement for a teenager, and she's a meticulous house-keeper.' Gabrielle thought of how the upturned trainers rudely marred the neat living-room.

'Any boyfriends?'

'There was a young man, Ethan, who tried to have a relationship with her but Jasmine got very withdrawn and wouldn't talk to him. When he persisted, she got really upset and put her fist through a window, which was quite a message. Even so, he's still her friend; she mentions him from time to time. I get the impression he's a bit on the fringes himself. He smokes weed and has some fairly dodgy mates so at times Jasmine's mixing with a rough crowd. I'm trying to get her to look at her safety and maybe choose better friends.'

'What kind of work has she done?'

'She worked at the fish factory and stuck at it for quite a few months, but processing fish is cold, wet, smelly work and they're often a tough crowd. They tease and bully. Jasmine, being so withdrawn, was an easy target and one day she snapped and threw a knife.'

Martina raised her eyebrows. 'So what happened?'

'She got the sack. And she was charged and fined, I think. She felt ashamed about it. I helped her get on a benefit because I feel she needs to be a bit stronger before she can take on earning a living. After all, most girls her age are still at school and in the care of their parents.'

'Do you think she could kill someone?'

'Physically, maybe. She's small but she's used to knives. But the knife-throwing incident was a one-off and she had been provoked for months. Emotionally? I doubt it. In therapy if she shows any anger she's quick to make excuses for the other person. She's more likely to take things out on herself. She has scars all up and down her arms from razor-cuts, the window incident, even some cigarette burns.'

Gabrielle paused and Martina seemed to read that there was something more. She waited with a quizzical look on her face.

'She was very angry about her father, how he abused those boys and was sent to jail, leaving her to pick up the pieces. She made no excuses for him.'

Martina looked thoughtful. 'Ok. Knife-throwing, mental instability, anger at her father...'

'I know, it doesn't look good.' Gabrielle took a deep breath. 'I didn't want to say this out loud, but I really think she might have done it. She looked so shocked and withdrawn in the Mental Health Unit.'

'Well, it does sound possible.'

'So what should I do to help her?'

'You? Nothing yet. We have to see what the police intend to do. If she's charged we'll need to know a lot more about the murder victim and how he died.'

Gabrielle noted the pronoun with a flutter of hope.

'My brother is probably doing the post-mortem.'

Martina looked amused. 'This is a small town. Tell me more.'

'Toby, my brother, is the pathologist. In fact, he's the one who suggested I get in touch with you. But he wouldn't tell me any more about the case, professional confidentiality and all that.'

Martina nodded. 'It all comes through the proper channels eventually. More coffee?'

'I've taken up a lot of your time already.'

'No problem, I have nothing planned for this evening and tomorrow's section of the workshop is under control. Would you like to show me a good place to have dinner?'

Gabrielle looked doubtful. She had planned to visit Jasmine again.

Martina held up her hands. 'It's ok, no pressure. I've enjoyed talking with you but of course you have a life here and plans of your own. Just recommend somewhere.'

Gabrielle gave her a surprised look. She hadn't thought of this sophisticated woman actually enjoying her company. 'I could have dinner with you if you'd like that. I just need to do a few things first. Can I meet you in, say, an hour?' She drew a map on a serviette and left with a smile.

Chapter Eight

Gabrielle was having a clothes crisis. She had suggested a cafe by the harbour and had phoned to book a table with a view of the sea. Aware that she was trying to make a good impression on Martina, she told herself that there was no need to over-compensate for Martina's qualifications. Even so, she had tried and rejected half her wardrobe. The little black dress joined the pile on the bed.

Finally she decided on black trousers, a burnt orange silk shirt and a tie-dyed scarf. Shoes? Definitely flat. She put her light brown hair up, then let it down again, then settled for a broad clip at the nape of her neck and some wispy bits around her face. She studied the effect. Even with her freckles dimmed by make-up it was more girlish than sophisticated. Pulling a face at herself in the mirror, she stuffed her wallet into a small black shoulder bag and headed off. Then came back for a squirt of perfume and another dab at her hair. She looked at her reflection in the mirror.

'You fancy her, don't you?' she said to herself. And replied firmly, 'Don't be silly, I hardly know her.'

Martina was already seated upstairs at the window when Gabrielle arrived. She looked up and smiled.

'I decided to walk so I left early. Great place. What a view!'

Gabrielle noted with relief that trousers and shirt had been a good bet. Martina was in black jeans and a slim-fitting red top.

They sat quietly for a moment, looking at the harbour and the shadowy shapes of the mountains across the bay. It was perfect timing, Gabrielle noted with satisfaction, as the clouds were taking on their sunset colours, from salmon pink to burnt orange, while the sky deepened from turquoise to navy blue. The trees on Haulashore Island were ragged black silhouettes and beyond the darkening sea the snowy caps of the mountains glowed pink in the last rays of the sun.

As they ordered, Martina issued a challenge. 'Let's see what they do here. I warn you, I eat out a lot in Wellington, so I'm not easy to please.'

Gabrielle smiled, quietly confident.

She told Martina that she had seen Jasmine again and it was good to know that she was out of bed and joining in the Unit's programme, but she still was not talking about her father's death. After a one-sided conversation with the teenager, Gabrielle had decided it was worse than talking to Aunt Lil, so she left. At least Aunt Lil tried to respond, even if she hardly made sense.

Martina was reassuring. 'There's nothing to be done at the moment and it's good to know that your client is in a safe place. The important thing is how to respond once the police make a move. And maybe they have someone else in their sights. You're anxious, understandably, but nothing bad has happened to her yet.'

'Apart from losing her father.'

'She'll have mixed feelings about that, of course, and probably some guilt because she has almost certainly wished him dead many times. You'll need to watch out for that.'

Gabrielle nodded. She didn't need to be told how to do her job.

Martina smiled. 'I'm sure you know all that. The main thing, if she is arrested, is for her to get a good lawyer and the lawyer can call me as an expert witness.'

'I know a very good woman lawyer here, Freda Bates, perhaps we could use her.'

'So that covers it for now. Enough shop?'

There was an awkward moment as both women realised they barely knew each other and had no idea what else to talk about. Silently hoping it would not sound too much as if she was interviewing the psychologist, Gabrielle set about finding out how Martina got into forensic psychology and what her family thought of her choice. She was thinking of her father's reaction to the suggestion that she, Gabrielle, might join the police. But Martina had had none of that. Her parents, a Hungarian immigrant and a New Zealand engineer, were keen only that she should get the best possible education. Her mother's wish was for her children to be doctors and a PhD, even in psychology, came close to satisfying that.

They were deep in conversation when the waiter hovered with their meals. They looked at each other's choices. Martina had a kingfish steak on saffron rice with an artistically dishevelled salad on the side. Gabrielle watched as the other woman sampled her food and when their eyes met over the second loaded forkful, they both grinned. The city-slicker approved. Pouring another glass of Chardonnay for each of them, Gabrielle applied herself to her bowl of fettuccine in creamy sauce, made bright with slices of pepper and cherry tomatoes.

Over gelato and sticky date pudding, Gabrielle found herself talking up her own family history as a fifth generation New Zealander and sharing her enthusiasm about her rural childhood. Growing up on the farm with her parents and Toby seemed like the best start she could have had.

'I was a bit of a tomboy because Toby and I were inseparable. Plus I was as mad about horses as a teenage girl can be. I did a bit of show-jumping and dressage but what I loved most was galloping over the paddocks. I miss that thrill.'

As they left the restaurant they were drawn towards the sea which shushed gently against the stone wall, the moon a silver path between the island and the Boulder Bank which formed the harbour. Anchored yachts swayed rhythmically as the waves lifted and dropped, lifted and dropped. They watched the waves quietly for a while, then returned to Gabrielle's car.

'It's been a lovely evening,' said Martina, as they drove round the port. 'Call me when you hear any developments in the case. And if you come to Wellington, get in touch, I'd like to return the favour.'

She leaned forward and for a giddy moment it seemed as though they would kiss, but Martina just gently tucked a stray wisp of hair behind

Gabrielle's ear. Then she slipped out of the car and walked briskly to the hotel entrance without looking back.

* * * * * *

Jasmine rocked back and forth so that her forehead hit the wall – *stop* – *stop* – *stop*.

Gabrielle's visit had reminded her of the night the police came to the house, asking them all questions till at the end of it Dad, big, strong, don't-bother-me-I'm-busy Dad, looked shrunken and lost for words as he walked between the officers to their car. That was the only time she had ever felt sorry for him. Later, when Susi ran away and Mum got into the brandy, she realised how he had dropped her in it and she got so angry with him that when he rang from jail she slammed the phone down and when Mum gave her a letter to post she tore it into little bits and dropped them down the stormwater drain.

The police had even taken her to the store room and asked if Dad had ever made a movie of her. Movies! She hardly had a photo of herself as a child, that's how much notice he took of her. She had always known he liked boys better. When boys came to the shop he gave them extra sweets and special smiles and never even looked at his own daughter.

Thump- thump – thump. A shout went up from the other side of the wall and suddenly Penny was in the room shaking her shoulder.

'Cut that out! You're winding up the guy in the next room and we just got him settled. Behave yourself or you'll have to have an injection.'

Was that a threat or a promise? thought Jasmine. It would be lovely to be wiped out for a few hours, but faced with an angry nurse she could only retreat inside herself. She lay down and faced the wall.

Chapter Nine

The woman sitting opposite was in her thirties, with crimson hair and a bright blue T-shirt with the legend 'All Girl' across her breasts. Her eyes were outlined in heavy black make-up. She was looking hard at her feet.

'I didn't intend to get involved with him,' said Lynley, miserably. 'She's my best friend, for God's sake. I'd never even looked at him in that way, but he came to pick me up when my car broke down. I texted Maree to say I was stuck out at Appleby and he just offered. I was so pleased to see him. He checked out the car and found the problem, loose wire or something, so he fixed it himself.'

'You were grateful that he rescued you?' suggested Gabrielle.

'Oh, yes, I told him he was a knight in shining armour. And he said if that's the case he deserved a kiss. Which, fair enough, he did.'

'So you gave him a kiss. Then what happened.'

'Well, I meant just to give him a little peck. But it was an amazing kiss, it just went on and on. Then we sat in the car right there on the side of the road, talking. I never met a guy who I could talk to so easily. I mean, I've known him for years, but he's different on his own. I really enjoyed talking to him.'

Gabrielle pictured Martina on the waterfront with the moonlight behind her. She pushed the thought away and paid attention.

'Who suggested things should go further?'

Lynley looked at her. 'I don't know. It just kind of happened. The sun came out and we walked down by the river and...' She smiled secretly to herself, then shook her head in reproof.

'Now I feel so guilty I can't look Maree in the face. She keeps asking what's wrong. I miss her, she's my mate. And he came round on his pub night with a bottle of wine as if it's all on now, every Thursday. And how do you say no when you've already said yes?'

'Do you want to say no?'

'I don't know!' Lynley grabbed a handful of tissues as tears burst the dam of her tough exterior.

Gabrielle sat quiet. She thought of and discarded several comments: 'We don't choose our feelings but we can choose what to do with them.' 'Friendship and loyalty are important.' 'Follow your heart.'

After a few moments she asked cautiously, 'If you could look into the future, say to this time next year, how do you see things turning out?'

In the silence that followed the question, Lynley's sobs subsided into sniffs. She blew her nose and took more tissues. She carefully wiped her eyes, avoiding the mascara, and took a deep breath.

'If I'm really honest?'

Gabrielle nodded. 'As honest as a crystal ball would be.'

'It all ends in tears. He would try to have his cake and eat it for a while, then he'd feel guilty and break it off. Probably tell Maree to try and make it ok. A year from now? I'd have lost both of them, and have a bad name among our friends.' She looked at Gabrielle.

'Does it seem worth it?' asked Gabrielle.

'You don't think about that at the time. Right now, of course it doesn't.'

She sighed. 'I'll have to tell him it's over. But if I get him to come round and talk about it we'll end up in bed for sure. One look and we're fired up.'

'Is there another way to break it off?'

'I'll have to phone him.'

Gabrielle could see the pain on Lynley's face. 'It's going to be hard, isn't it?'

Lynley reached for the tissues again and wiped away the tears which leaked silently over her eyeliner.

'You'll need something to help you to stay strong. What would help?'

Lynley gave a small, twisted smile. 'I'll think of you saying "be as honest as a crystal ball, how does it turn out?"' she said.

Gabrielle smiled at her. 'Ok, I hope that can help. Because it does sound as if you'd be the one left sad and lonely. Maybe if you stop now, before you get too attached, it might be easier.'

'And I'll feel better if I'm the one who breaks it off.'

The tough persona returned as Lynley prepared herself to face the world. She took one more tissue and carefully wiped under her eyes. Then she stood up and brushed her skirt down briskly.

'Same time next week?'

Gabrielle nodded. 'Take care.'

As the door shut she stared out the window, thinking of the risks people took for just a little human connection. It had been a long time since she took any such risk. Had her fingers really been burnt so badly?

She reached a decision, picked up the phone and dialled.

'Martina's answer-phone, leave a message.'

'Hi, it's me, Gabrielle. I'm thinking of coming up to Wellington for the weekend. Give me a call if it's possible to meet up.'

Her heart was beating a little faster as she hung up.

Time for a break. She made a sandwich and a cup of coffee and took her lunch out into the garden. She looked at the results of her work and began to plan the next tasks. Definitely time for some pruning and maybe some more winter-flowering annuals. She had just got up to fetch her gardening book when the door bell rang.

On the doorstep was Detective Walt Parker with a file in his hand.

'Can I come in? I need to ask you some questions about Jasmine Lawson.'

Gabrielle led him into the counselling room. He had on the same tweed jacket, and out of the office he looked even more like a farmer than a policeman, so that she glanced out to the street, half-expecting to see a ute with a Border Collie standing alert in the back. But it was the usual 'unmarked' white sedan.

Parker was asking about her work with Jasmine. He had a surprisingly deep voice which he used softly in a way which could be taken as either engaging or menacing. Iron fist in a sheepskin glove, thought Gabrielle.

She explained, much as she had done for Martina, how she came to be seeing Jasmine as a client and how long she had known her. There was no point fudging any of that, Detective Parker had the notes and Gabrielle had been well trained – she took a thorough history and wrote it all down.

'Let's just go through it all step by step,' he said. Gabrielle recognised the non-committal tone she herself used with clients at times, and she noted how strange it felt to have the roles reversed.

'So she was left at home with her mother when her father went to jail. There don't seem to be any references in your notes to how she felt about that,' he said. He opened the file. 'But there does seem to be a page missing. The notes stop mid-sentence here.'

Gabrielle leaned over and had a look, trying to be vague. 'So it does. I must have been interrupted.'

'Hmm, the rest of the file looks very professional. You wouldn't have destroyed any notes would you?'

Gabrielle avoided looking at the bottom drawer. She knew she was not a good liar.

'We were trained to be thorough,' she said truthfully, smiling at him. 'I wouldn't destroy my notes.' Her heart beat faster and she hoped she was not blushing.

'So what was Jasmine's attitude to her father?' Parker seemed to be following his own line of thought.

'She didn't talk about him much. One thing about working with teenagers is that they're very immediate. She had a lot on her plate trying to live independently and protect herself from her mother's demands. I was mainly working on her safety in a day to day sense.'

'Did he abuse her?'

'She has always denied it. I couldn't confront her about that without losing the rapport that was necessary to continue therapy so I'd have to say we didn't really talk about that.'

'It sounds as if you think he might have,' the detective persisted.

'As I said, we didn't talk about it. I don't think I should speculate.'

'I understand it's part of the therapy to arrange for the victim to confront the perpetrator. Had you discussed that?' He was watching her with a shrewd look, as if he knew the answer.

'Of course not, we hadn't even talked about the fact that he might have abused her. He might not have either. And anyway as far as I knew he was still in jail.' Gabrielle could definitely feel her face getting hot now.

'I am right though, that would have been the next step?'

'It's one of the possibilities. I'm careful to sound out the client and to make sure that will be beneficial and not make things worse.'

'So you didn't encourage her to write to him in jail? He had the letter on him.'

This time her face surely betrayed her astonishment, which Parker noted with a slight nod.

He continued, 'Would you say she could become enraged?'

'Angry, briefly. But it fizzled out very quickly and she usually made excuses for other people.'

'The letter was pretty angry. And she does have a conviction for throwing a knife at a fellow-worker.'

Gabrielle sighed. 'That's going to haunt her, isn't it? There was a lot of provocation there.'

'And what if she was under the influence of alcohol or drugs? How might she react then?'

'She was totally against alcohol because of her mother's addiction. I don't know that she would use drugs either.'

'The hospital found quite a cocktail in her blood tests,' he told her. 'Besides, she has some friends who are well-known for their drug use and at least one young man thought she could supply him with cannabis.'

Gabrielle opened her mouth, realised there was nothing useful she could say, and closed it again.

Walt Parker smiled privately, closed his notebook and stood up. 'Thank you for your help.'

He held out his hand and Gabrielle shook it. After she had showed him out, she sat for a while at her desk, staring into the garden without really seeing it. The counselling tutors had warned their students that there are three kinds of information: what your client tells you, what you know they are not telling you and what you don't know they are not telling you. The skill and the danger lie in the third category: what you don't know you don't know.

There could be a lot she didn't know about Jasmine.

* * * * * *

It really was chance that she saw Crystal at the supermarket later that afternoon, though she did abandon her trolley in the bakery aisle to follow her sister-in-law out into the car park. She caught up with her just as she was struggling to open the boot with Zoe in one arm and the shopping in the other.

'Hi, Crystal, let me.' Gabrielle opened the boot and helped her put the bags of groceries in.

'Awful case Toby's been on, isn't it?' she said casually as Crystal put Zoe in her car seat. 'Must be distressing for him.'

'He takes it pretty calmly but I know it upsets him. It was extra yuk this time – the man was a mess. Not a bone in his face left intact. I said, I don't know how you stand it. He said it's interesting, like a jig-saw puzzle.'

'Putting the face back together?' Gabrielle was shocked.

'No, working out what happened. He likes that part. You know, they hit him in the face over and over and then stabbed him to death.'

Gabrielle nodded sympathetically.

'How can anyone be so vicious? I try to listen to Toby, I know he has to off-load, but sometimes the details stick in my head.'

Crystal looked so upset that Gabrielle regretted bringing the matter up. She put a hand on her arm.

'I'm sorry I made you think about it. Don't go there, think of something else.' Zoe was whimpering and tugging at her mother's top. 'How's my lovely niece today?'

Crystal smiled. 'She's hungry. Better get home and put some dinner on, eh sweetheart?' She smiled at the little girl in the car seat and Zoe chuckled, pleased to see her mother happy again. Gabrielle reached in and stroked the white-blonde curls.

'See you soon.'

Crystal opened the driver's door. 'Yes, come for dinner sometime. It was good to see you the other night.'

Gabrielle stood in the car park for a few minutes, then she got in her car and drove home, completely forgetting to finish her shopping. She felt bad about having an ulterior motive for getting information out of her sister-in-law and resolved to make up for it by visiting Crystal and Zoe, or maybe taking them out for lunch. She thought of her vibrant little niece with the usual pangs of love and sadness.

Chapter Ten

Supervison reminded Gabrielle of her childhood, when her Catholic family all went to confession on Saturday evening to prepare for Mass on Sunday. There was the examination of conscience and the submission to authority, as well as the anticipation of the feedback her supervisor would give her and the changes she might expect her to make: the 'firm purpose of amendment.' She liked Rona and knew her well, but she was somewhat in awe of her. For one thing, she was one of few Maori counsellors in the area and for another she was a woman in her sixties with a great deal of life experience.

Rona had come to the course as a guest tutor and challenged the students about their white middle-class backgrounds and ivory tower view of therapy. She particularly challenged their belief that they were learning a holistic therapy. Gabrielle had welcomed the opportunity to develop these ideas but at first Rona wouldn't take her on as a supervisee. She had told her to come back when she was less wet behind the ears and although Gabrielle hadn't liked to hear that, from where she stood now she could see how starry-eyed she had been when she first graduated. Therapy had been such a revelation for her, she was like a convert trying to share the good news with everyone. After a couple of years in practice she had approached Rona again and become her supervisee, continuing to be moved by something centred and enduring about Rona.

This time, Gabrielle knew she had gone out on a limb. If she examined her conscience she could find boundary breaches a flock of sheep could get through.

As a result, she arrived at Rona's house with not just butterflies but a whole ecosystem cavorting in her abdomen.

Rona was a flax weaver as well as a therapist. Two kits, which her deft fingers had plaited in gold and red diamond patterns, hung from a hook on the back of the door. A korowai with a dense pattern of blue and white feathers was spread on one wall. Gabrielle knew that the cloak was a family heirloom because she had asked Rona about it. It had been woven by Rona's grandmother, a great artist, and the feathers were pukeko and albatross, each one woven into the flax individually. It was very delicate and used only for the most important ceremonial occasions. Rona had said that when she died the korowai would cover her coffin as she was carried from the meeting house.

Gabrielle took her supervisor's hand and kissed her on the cheek in greeting, then settled herself on the sofa. It was covered with a multi-coloured crocheted blanket of the kind which she would usually associate with working-class grandmothers. Somehow in this room it seemed exotic, a foil to the weaving and the red-painted walls. Beside her on a low, carved table was a small basket, also Rona's work, filled with shells and pebbles. Gabrielle felt the room calm her and embrace her.

In her big chair on the other side of the room Rona waited for Gabrielle to begin.

'A lot has happened this past couple of weeks.' *Bless me, for I have sinned,* Gabrielle thought and ploughed on.

'Do you remember me talking about Jasmine, the teenager whose father is in jail for sexually abusing young boys?'

'Ae,' Rona nodded.

'Well, I went to her flat because she didn't turn up for her appointment and I found her father dead on the floor.' Her voice seemed to stick and she could not say any more. The body on the floor flashed into her mind as vividly as if she was standing in the flat right at this moment.

Rona was studying her face with a concerned look. 'That's a very disturbing thing for you to discover. What are you feeling about it?'

'I feel guilty, I should never have gone there. I wish I had just waited; someone would have got hold of me to tell me where she was. I just wish I hadn't been there.' She put her hand over her mouth. 'That's awful, isn't it? Like wanting to hide my head in the sand.'

'Not so surprising. Who would want to be part of something terrible? What had happened to the man?'

'That's what makes it so awful. He was lying in a pool of blood. The police immediately called for the homicide team so obviously they thought it was murder. I don't know exactly how he died but Jasmine cut her wrists after that and is in the Mental Health Unit. She's not saying much. What if it was her? '

Rona asked, 'Could it be her? What would that mean for you?'

While Gabrielle thought about the question, Rona picked up on her hesitation.

'There's something you feel bad about.'

Gabrielle looked up sharply. She didn't miss much.

'It's like Pandora's box. The situation has escaped out of the safety of my quiet therapy room and I'm out there too, doing things that are way beyond my brief.'

Gabrielle decided to confess. She explained to Rona about talking to Toby and meeting Martina, and about tricking Crystal into telling her how Don had died. She didn't mention the notes.

'Would you do this for any one of your clients or is this young woman special in some way?'

That 'special' question again. It took the matter to another level, one that Gabrielle didn't really want to go to.

'None of my other clients have needed so much help. But there's something vulnerable and also courageous about her. She hasn't had much of a start in life but she has potential.'

'Maybe there's a bit of your ego involved in being the one to transform her, to bind her to you with gratitude.'

Gabrielle shook her head. 'I don't think I expect to get anything out of this, except the pleasure of seeing her get on with her life. It feels, kind of, well – motherly.'

Rona, a foster-mother of several children herself, smiled.

'That's a noble feeling but you're not her mother and she'll have no loyalty to you.'

Gabrielle winced. 'I'm not anyone's mother.'

Rona nodded. 'I know. Neither am I, strictly speaking, but the kids I've raised have been a great joy as well as a great heartbreak over the years. I do understand how that motherly feeling wants to find expression. But it makes you vulnerable if you act on it.'

'I've met her mother. She's as hard as nails – no comfort for Jasmine there. And she blamed me for getting involved.'

'However tough things are, family is family. They stick together and resent the outsider, especially one who knows their secrets. So what have you planned next for this young woman?'

'I don't know that there's anything else I can do,' Gabrielle replied. 'Freda Bates will be her lawyer and Martina Day will help as an expert witness. I just have to hope the police will look at other possibilities. I feel there's a piece of the puzzle missing and I'm going round and round trying to think what it could be.'

'It sounds as if you've taken a crash course in criminal defence in the last couple of weeks. Perhaps you should leave it to the experts now.'

'Everyone says that, but I feel I need to get just one more piece of the puzzle. It's as if it's just beyond my fingertips. Maybe then I can hand it over. And I do feel strongly about visiting her in the Unit because I doubt her mother will go there much and who else will be there for her if I abandon her?'

'Now,' said Rona, 'you mentioned meeting this Martina and I noticed you blushed. Is she special too?'

Another bull's-eye for the wise woman.

Gabrielle grinned ruefully. 'Probably but I need a bit more time on this one.' She shook her head. 'Why are all these things happening to me? It used to be so straightforward – therapy room, clients here,' she mimed a pile on one side of her chair, 'and home, my life and friends here,' and she made a pile on the other side.

Rona smiled. 'Nice if you can get it, but you've been in practice a few years now. Inevitably things start to overlap. We Maori are more used to finding people in multiple roles because there are not so many of us and we have lots of inter-relationships. The challenge is to stay clear and honest with yourself and the others.'

'So what do I do now?'

'You're maturing as a counsellor and things aren't so black and white any more. Your values are being tested. I'm not saying what's right or wrong, you have to work that out. Go with your gut feeling, Gabrielle, but find a safe way to do it.'

After leaving Rona's place Gabrielle parked her car at Queens Gardens and walked around among the trees for a while, looking at the last of the roses and the absurd little boy fountain. Then she sat by the pond to watch the swans. She wondered what swans thought about. Very little, probably, they seemed too tranquil to have much on their minds as they paddled slowly from one end of the pond to the other. They looked like a pair but she had read in the paper that the area was too small for breeding so two males had been chosen. Maybe they were gay: appropriate for the Queens Gardens. Gabrielle allowed herself a pale smile.

* * * * * *

Dodging Heidi, whom she could see making a beeline for her from across the lounge, Gabrielle went straight to the nurses' station to ask Barry how Jasmine was doing. He had the day off, she found, and the young doctor was nowhere to be seen, so she introduced herself to Penny who was now Jasmine's nurse.

Penny led off in a different direction and when Gabrielle queried this she said, 'Oh didn't you know? She's in the secure unit now, since she's been charged.'

Gabrielle stopped in the middle of the corridor. 'Charged?'

'With her father's murder.' Penny sounded very matter-of-fact.

'How is she taking that?'

'Much the same.'

Gabrielle didn't know what to make of her off-hand tone of voice. Perhaps for the nurses here this was all in a day's work.

They continued down the corridor and Penny unlocked a door.

Gabrielle stepped into a room which was entirely covered in a kind of peach-coloured vinyl – the floor, the walls and a platform where a mattress lay, creating a bed where Jasmine was lay.

'Jasmine, your counsellor's here to see you,' said Penny and to Gabrielle, 'I'll have to lock you in. Press this to call me.' She pointed to a button set into the wall, then she left. The lock gave a solid 'clunk'.

Jasmine had not moved. There was the faint sound of piped music, perhaps the local radio station. Somewhere down the corridor she could hear a male voice calling out monotonously, 'Get me a smoke will you? Get me a bloody smoke.' Another nearby replied, 'Shut the fuck up.' They kept it up, antiphon and refrain, with the doggedness of the truly bored.

Gabrielle sat at the end of the sleeping platform and looked around her. All the corners of the room were rounded and there were no sharp edges, no other furniture. The window was double-glazed and couldn't be opened.

After a few moments Jasmine drew herself into sitting position and wrapped her arms around her knees. She was wearing a rather shapeless tracksuit and her hair looked stringy and unwashed. Without her usual mascara her face looked wan and younger than ever. She dragged a quilt over her bare feet.

'So how are you?' asked Gabrielle.

'They think I killed my father. How would I be?' Jasmine's tone was sullen and flat.

Gabrielle nodded. 'I found him when I went looking for you. What do you think happened?'

Jasmine's eyes remained dull. 'I can't remember. I would remember if I did something so terrible, wouldn't I?'

This revelation worried Gabrielle. 'Sometimes people forget terrible things,' she said. 'But when you told me you hated him, it wasn't that you wanted him dead, was it? It seemed that you wanted him to admit that what he'd done had turned out very hard on you. You wanted him to take responsibility for it.'

'Well, the detective says I did it.' The despair in her voice was so total it sounded as if the teenager would go down for the crime because she did not care what happened to her.

Gabriélle thought of Walt Parker and remembered something. 'Detective Parker said that you wrote to your Dad.'

'I wanted to tell him what I thought of him and how what he did turned out for me. And to make him understand that I had to leave Mum. I couldn't keep looking after her like he told me to. It was making me crazy. I had to go, so it wasn't my fault I broke my promise.'

Jasmine burst into tears and buried her face in her hands. Her sobs shook her thin shoulders as Gabrielle put a hand on her back and murmured soothingly until she could speak again. Some emotion was definitely better than that terrible passivity.

'What did you want from him?' she asked the young woman.

Tears threatened to overwhelm Jasmine again but she sniffed loudly and said, 'I just wanted him to admit what he'd done and say he was sorry. Just to write back, I didn't want to see him. I got a letter from the police saying he would be released in March and they gave the address in Christchurch where he would have to live. I never thought he'd dare show his face in this town where everyone hates him.'

Gabrielle kept her hand on the girl's bird-boned back as if to maintain a line of communication between them. She could feel the gulp of indrawn breath.

'Then he just turned up. He was all lovey-dovey, wanted me to forgive him, give him a place to stay. Yuk. I was getting really creeped out and I nearly let him in then I thought of what you said about sticking up for myself. So I told him to bugger off, he ruined my life once, he wasn't going to ruin it again. He just laughed and walked past me and sat down. He said he'd come to see me and he wasn't going anywhere. I screamed at him but he wouldn't move. I left him there and went round to Ethan's place.'

'That's Ethan who was your boyfriend?'

'My friend. He understands about Dad. I told him I'd yelled at Dad and he was really proud of me for sticking up for myself. We talked about what next, like going to the cops or whatever. Then this guy Davey arrived, I knew him from school, though he was a bit older. Ethan told him my name and he laughed and said "So that old paedophile's your Dad, eh?" '

Jasmine looked up. 'I hated Davey for saying it but that's what he is. He deserved everything that happened to him.'

Gabrielle winced. 'Just don't say that too loudly. So what happened that night at Ethan's place ...?'

'Davey went away and came back with his mate and some stuff. I got out of it. I don't remember.' Jasmine hid her face again. Gabrielle decided not to press her, for fear she would shut down again.

'What's it like in here?'

'Not as bad as I thought. The food's terrible, I'll be fat by the time I leave here. And there's nothing to do, especially now I'm locked up. I miss the beach. And my mates.'

'I'd like to talk to Ethan. He might know something which will help you. Where would I find him?'

Jasmine gave an address which Gabrielle wrote down. 'Tell him to visit me, I'm going even more mad from boredom.'

'I brought you something to read, I hope you like detective stories. Nothing gruesome, I promise, it's an art theft.'

She handed Jasmine the book. As she turned to go Jasmine said, 'I've still got this.' She held out her hand. In her palm lay a smooth white stone.

Gabrielle smiled. 'I'm glad. I hope it helps you to stay strong.'

She pressed the buzzer and after a while heard the key turn in the lock. Penny escorted her down the corridor and as she left the nurse said, 'She'll be in court tomorrow to enter her plea. Just thought you should know.'

* * * * * *

Jasmine lay back on the stupid bed. The blankets were scratchy things, stitched over and over so that you couldn't rip them up and get strips to hang yourself. Everything in the room was designed to be suicide-proof but she had her plan. She thought back over what she had said to Gabrielle and a sick feeling came over her. She'd said too much. Gabrielle acted all caring, as if she was on your side but she would go to the police or the nurses, she was one of them. Sneaky how she used that counsellor face and long silences to get stuff out of you.

She curled up on her side and hugged her knees, rocking a little to ease the pain in her belly. She tried to count but her breath came in uneven gasps.

She can hear her father saying, 'I'll do it. You'll bruise her again.'

Her mother answers crossly, 'She bruises easily. They didn't need to make such a fuss.'

'I'll do it.'

He calls Jasmine and takes her by the arm to the bathroom.

'Bend down.'

She squats, puzzled. Mum just flies at her with the wooden spoon, screaming. He arranges her, bottom up, hands splayed like pale starfish on the floor. He's never spanked her before. He lifts her skirt and with finger and thumb he gently pulls down her teddy bear knickers. She can feel his breath on her bottom...

Her starfish hands are white knuckled. He pulls up the teddy bears with a snap of elastic.

'Go to your room.'

She runs, through the kitchen and into her room where she curls up on the bed. Ears like antennae listen for where Dad is. After a while he comes out of the bathroom and goes into the kitchen.

Mum shouts at him, 'That wasn't a spanking, she didn't even cry. You're useless.'

He shoulders past her and Jasmine hears the front door slam. Mum's footsteps stamp down the hall to Jasmine's bedroom.

Chapter Eleven

The sun was down behind the hills, casting blood-red streaks over dirty clouds, when Gabrielle pulled up in the street where Jasmine had told her Ethan lived. It seemed an improbable place for a house, an industrial area which was emptying as people left their workplaces and headed home. She parked the car and walked along the pavement past a panel beater's yard and a wood and coal merchant. Not many places showed their street numbers but she glimpsed a battered letterbox behind a small furniture manufacturer. Beside it a narrow path led to a house sited well back from the road. She walked up the path, alert to the possibility of unfriendly dogs. The way became dank and muddy, then turned sharply to lead across a small square of concrete to the back door of the house. She knocked. Nothing happened. She knocked again. A dog barked once. A male voice called out, 'Someone get the bloody door, will you.' Footsteps approached and the door was wrenched open.

'Yes...?' A thin young man stood there in jeans and a T-shirt, barefoot, holding back a suspicious-looking dog which growled in a low murmur. Beyond him, Gabrielle could see a kitchen bench piled high with dishes and through the next doorway a darkened living-room with ill-defined shapes lurking in the gloom.

'I'm looking for Ethan,' she said.

'I'm Ethan,' the young man answered.

'I'm Gabrielle, I've got a message from Jasmine. Can we talk a minute?'

Ethan looked towards the gloom inside. 'The guys are in the lounge.'

'Could we go for a walk, maybe?'

This seemed to strike the young man as an excellent idea. He grinned faintly and nodded. 'I'll get my shoes.'

He closed the door and Gabrielle stepped back into the little yard, relieved not to have to enter the foetid flat. Ethan came back wearing battered trainers and rolling a cigarette. The dog followed eagerly. Ethan snapped his fingers and it came to heel as they set off down the path.

'How did you hear from Jasmine? Is she ok?'

Gabrielle described the Mental Health Unit and how she had visited Jasmine there.

'It sounds better than prison,' was his response.

'Well, prison might be next unless she has some help. What happened? Can you tell me?'

'She was pretty wild about her Dad turning up so she came round to my place.'

Gabrielle nodded and Ethan continued, 'She got totally off her face.'

'So she said. Tell me about it.'

'Well, Davey was here, that was in the afternoon. When he said some stuff about Don, Jasmine was really mad. She cried and then she yelled and swore. Then she demanded some weed. So we had a smoke but that didn't calm her down, she yelled some more and started throwing things around. The guys told me to take her away if I couldn't stop her so we went down the back beach with Nasty here.'

The dog pricked up his ears, no doubt thinking the combination of 'beach' and 'Nasty' a good thing.

'Did that help?'

'Yeah, we walked a bit and she calmed down. But it was getting dark so we went back and the guys were passing round weed and spirits and stuff. She wanted to join in. I didn't think she should but she got mad and said I didn't have to babysit her.'

'Then what?'

'She didn't get angry again, she had some stuff and got kind of quiet. The next bit I've told the police about it. We all crashed, Jas slept on the couch. In the morning this Indian guy came round banging on the door, making a hell of a racket. It was still real early too. Someone let him in and he tried to wake Jas up and that's when we saw all the blood. I called the ambulance.'

Gabrielle noticed a twitch in Ethan's jaw. 'Who is that guy? At the Unit they called him Jasmine's boyfriend.'

Ethan snorted. 'He wishes. Hangs around like a bad smell. Ram he's called. Better not act like one, is all I can say.'

Nasty whined a little in sympathy and pushed his nose into Ethan's hand.

'So how does this Ram fit in?' She didn't like to make Ethan any more jealous by going on about him but she really wanted to know.

'He chatted Jasmine up over coffee one time, just walked into the Copper Kettle like he owned the place and sat down with her. Asked her where he could get some weed and like a muppet I gave her some for him. He's been hanging round ever since.'

'So who were the other guys – Davey and who else? Maybe if they talk to the police they can help Jasmine.'

'They're not exactly helpful types and they certainly don't help the police. I wouldn't go calling on them if I were you.'

'Just a name then?'

' Try Spaz. He's the least worst, if you know what I mean. He lives in a sleep-out up the valley, behind the big old house. ' He described the place.

Gabrielle wrote it down. 'I can't call him Spaz. What's his real name?'

' Everyone calls him Spaz. He walks funny 'cause he fried his brain with drugs. He's a bit simple but he's harmless.'

They walked back towards the car and Gabrielle told Ethan how to get to the Unit if he wanted to see Jasmine.

'She can have visitors then?' he asked.

'Maybe phone ahead, but yes I think so.'

Ethan nodded. 'I'll go and see her.'

'You're a good friend to stick by her.' Gabrielle got into the car.

Ethan bent down to the window. 'I always feel bad 'cause I put her old man away and that made life tough for her, you know. My Mum said it would be for the best, but it hasn't turned out so good for any of us.'

Gabrielle stared.

'Didn't you know? I'm the one that blew the whistle.'

* * * * * *

Gabrielle rearranged her morning, thinking it would be good for Jasmine see a friendly face in court. Outside the courtroom some of the day's customers were having a last minute nervous cigarette. Gabrielle walked up the steps and took a seat in the waiting-room where the sun streamed in to light up the wooden panelling and the cheap vinyl chairs. A mix of people waited too. Some had family and friends for support; one or two stood looking out the window, obviously alone. After a while Gabrielle began to see who was who. The lawyers were easy to pick, dashing up the stairs with industrial strength briefcases and uniform black suits. The defendants looked nervous and very tidy. Their supporters were in casual clothes and were looking around or chatting to each other. One neatly dressed woman was a puzzle until a lawyer called her into a side room, and Gabrielle decided that she must be a witness. Sitting there without a role made Gabrielle feel as if she'd gate-crashed a funeral.

She was relieved when the clerk opened the doors and she could go in and take a seat in the back row of the small public gallery with a few other supporters. At the far end she could see the reporter from the local paper, notebook poised. Jasmine's mother came in, noticed Gabrielle and sat as far from her as the small space allowed. In the hushed atmosphere everyone sat, subdued in their Sunday best, waiting to begin.

In front of the public gallery, lawyers sat at desks and fossicked in their files and briefcases, Freda among them. Her stylishly streaked hair and purple-framed glasses contrasted with her sober black jacket which she wore with trousers and flat square-toed shoes. When she turned Gabrielle could see the emerald green of her shirt. There was something capable and slightly subversive about her, as if she didn't buy into the stereotypes of her job. She caught Gabrielle's eye with a slight nod which was reassuring.

'All rise.'

The judge, a middle-aged woman in a smart black suit, took her place on the bench and the clerk ushered the first person into the dock. The young man, hair still wet from his shower, looked like a rabbit caught in the headlights. Driving while under the influence of alcohol. Guilty. Bailed for sentencing. A young woman, who seemed unable to find the dock until the clerk walked her over to it – theft as a servant. An older man – burglary, his profession perhaps, since he looked resigned rather than intimidated.

At this point two men came into the public gallery. One, with ragged fair hair and black denims, brushed past Gabrielle to get to a seat. He hissed at his mate, ' Psst, Davey, ' to indicate that he should follow. Davey's leathers smelled of grease and sweat as he pushed through to the next seat. He sat almost touching Gabrielle's elbow but his attention was on the dock.

A police officer brought Jasmine through a door at the back of the courtroom. With her hair scraped back in a tight pony tail and dressed in what might have been her mother's best clothes, a dark skirt and jacket, she looked translucently pale She gripped the edge of the dock and swayed a little when the police prosecutor read from his charge sheet.

The judge addressed her. 'You are charged with murder, how do you plead?'

Freda stood and spoke for her, 'Not guilty, ma'am.'

She was remanded to the Mental Health Unit for a psychiatrist's report. Freda asked for bail and it was denied on the grounds of Jasmine's previous conviction for assault. The knife-throwing incident in the fish factory had already come back to haunt her. The judge spoke quietly in a matter-of-fact tone which did not permit argument so it was all over very quickly. Jasmine was led away by a uniformed officer and Freda followed her through the back door which was off limits to the public. Gabrielle left the courtroom, giving a slight bow towards the judge as she had seen the lawyers do. She hovered in the foyer, hoping to see Freda and maybe even to let Jasmine know she was there.

Kathy came out of a side door and they said simultaneously, 'Hello, what are you doing here?'

Kathy answered first. 'Just arranging for a client to pay off her fines. We're done, I was on my way back to the Women's Centre. What about you?'

'Supporting the client I told you about. She's been remanded to the Unit.'

'So you've been seeing Jasmine? They were talking about her at the Centre this morning. I guessed that was who you meant the other day.'

Gabrielle felt shocked that her attempt at confidentiality was so transparent. 'How do you know her?'

'Oh she's often at the Centre. Since she's been unemployed, she's been doing our art course. She's pretty good too.'

Before Gabrielle could respond Davey and his mate clattered through the foyer and mounted a motorbike which was illegally parked on the grass near the steps. They roared off, Davey driving and his mate's unhelmeted hair flying in the slipstream.

Kathy stared after them. 'What are those ratbags up to?'

'I think they came to support Jasmine too – they were in the courtroom while she entered her plea.'

Kathy snorted. 'I doubt "support" is in their vocabulary. They'll be up to something. We tried to get Jasmine to stay away from that crowd, they're pure trouble, "Pure" being the operative word.'

Gabrielle looked at her with a puzzled smile.

'You missed my pun? Girl, you're getting out of touch, beavering away behind closed doors as you do. "Pure" is pure methamphetamine, otherwise known as "P". Those guys are serious druggies, and probably dealers. You should come back and do some shifts at the Women's Centre, like you did when you were a student. Get back in touch with the real world.'

Gabrielle grinned at her. 'If the real world involves up-to-date knowledge of drug terminology, I'll have to think about it. There's something else though...'

Just then Freda came through the foyer and left via the main doors.

'Honey, I've got to dash, I'm hoping to catch Freda. Talk to you soon, eh?'

Gabrielle cut across the car park and intercepted Freda.

'That was over quickly. What happens now?' she asked.

Freda looked relaxed and confident. Clearly, to her, the appearance was a minor step in a familiar routine.

'She'll go back to the secure unit until the case comes to trial. The psychiatrist will make a full assessment and report to the court in a month's time, then a date will be set for depositions. It could be three or four months before she comes back to court.'

Gabrielle was horrified. 'She's out of her mind with boredom already, and she was fragile to start with. Three or four months in that place will be hell for her.'

'That's how it has to be in the meantime. Maybe the psychiatrist will recommend some alternative.'

Gabrielle couldn't understand how she could be so casual about it. If the wheels of justice were to do their slow grind, it looked as if it was up to Gabrielle to help Jasmine – she needed to be released from that dreadful place urgently.

But before she could say more, Freda put a reassuring hand on her arm. 'Don't look so worried. This is just the beginning and you have to trust me to do my job. It's great she has the support of someone who cares so much about her and you can really help her best by keeping in touch. I know she'll appreciate it.'

She smiled, a smile which softened and lit up her face and even, Gabrielle couldn't help noticing, made a dimple in her left cheek. Then with another pat on the arm, she turned and walked briskly away.

Chapter Twelve

Gabrielle waited for the woman opposite her to speak. Rosemary was in her forties, neatly turned out in shades of green, her grey hair crisply cut and her make-up perfect. She sat very still with her ankles crossed and her hands in her lap.

Her husband had died suddenly about a year ago and she had sought out counselling recently because her friends had grown worried about her. They had distressed Rosemary by suggesting that it was time to move on, which Rosemary interpreted as meaning that she should forget Athol, her husband of twenty years.

Over the first few sessions, Gabrielle had built up a picture of their marriage. Athol was fifteen years older than Rosemary, a colonel in the army who liked his home run as precisely as his barracks. Whatever romance had blossomed between them in their early years had become a husk, held together by routine and obedience. Rosemary had continued after his death as if he were about to reappear at any moment and would be affronted by dereliction of duty. Gabrielle could see why the friends were worried: the widow had not yet shown any signs of evolving into the independent woman she now could be.

Often, when working with a client who was grieving for the loss of someone close to them, Gabrielle would talk about the dead person in the present tense and make them an active presence in the living person's life. For many the process of greeting and embracing the dear one they had lost had a healing effect which allowed them to move on but, for

Rosemary, Athol was too present, controlling her even from the afterlife. Something different was needed.

Gabrielle reached for a picture she had pinned on the wall. It was taken from a child's school book and showed the life cycle of the Monarch butterfly. At the top of the circle was the white dot of the egg, to the right the striped caterpillar, at the bottom the chrysalis with its row of gold stitching, and on the left the butterfly itself, its triumphant orange and black wings patterned like stained glass.

She passed the picture to Rosemary.

'Do you remember this?'

Rosemary nodded. 'We did it at school. Didn't everyone?'

'Where do you think you are in the cycle at the moment?'

Rosemary studied the diagram. She was drawn to the beautiful butterfly, but she shook her head. Her hand hovered over the caterpillar. Then she pointed to the chrysalis and looked up at Gabrielle.

Gabrielle smiled and nodded. 'It's a time when you are going through a change, isn't it? Life after Athol is going to be different but you don't know in what way.'

'I'd be fine if things stayed the same.'

'They don't though, do they? Things always change and going through the transition isn't easy. We can pull all the familiar things around us, wrap them tight like the chrysalis and try to stay safe, but the changes will go on whether we like it or not. What's your chrysalis made of?'

Rosemary thought about it. 'Just keeping to the routine, doing things the way Athol liked them to be done. And not letting my appearance go, because he liked to be proud of me in public.'

'And what's happening inside the chrysalis?'

Tears came into Rosemary's eyes. 'I don't know.'

'That's it. The caterpillar doesn't go into the chrysalis thinking "I'll just pop in here and grow some long legs and some nice orange wings." It wraps itself up tight and safe and then it melts down completely, it turns into a kind of soup. Then Nature builds the butterfly out of the soup. That must take a lot of faith on the part of the caterpillar.'

Rosemary said, 'I don't think they have enough brain to worry about it.'

Gabrielle smiled. 'Lucky them, eh? That's where people have so much more trouble with change. We don't like being soup, we like to have things under control. So transitions are rough on us, it can be hard to have faith and let Nature take her course.'

They talked a little more about change, but Gabrielle knew not to push things too hard. Rosemary would need time to let the image of the chrysalis, with its message of potential, sink in.

As the session ended Gabrielle said, 'Therapy can be like a chrysalis. Coming here is a kind of container, while change takes place. That way you don't have to work so hard at keeping it all together, I can share the job with you.'

After the last client of the day, Gabrielle decided to take Lil for a drive. A light breeze treated the white clouds like tufts of wool, teasing them out and tossing the shreds across the sky. As they left the rest home, she turned the car towards the main road and headed out of town. Aunt Lil seemed to find the movement soothing and she settled cosily into her seat. After a few minutes Gabrielle glanced over, expecting to see her aunt dozing there, but Lil's face was alert.

'Cows,' she said, with a note of approval, as they passed a farm.

'I thought we could have a look at the beach today,' Gabrielle told her. 'The wind's a bit cold but it's such a lovely day. You might even like to go for a walk.'

Lil did not reply and Gabrielle turned on the radio. A cello piece filled the car, as plaintive as a human voice, and although Lil made no response, Gabrielle hoped she could still enjoy music.

She drove over a bridge and through the pine trees of Rabbit Island, parking almost at the water's edge so that they could look at the sea. Where the waves made a frill of foam two or three people walked their dogs and a man and a boy strained against a huge kite. Right in front of the car a Labrador ran, barking, up to a fat corgi.

'Don't be a bully,' said Lil.

Gabrielle smiled at her. Any sign that she was aware of what was going on around her was a pleasure these days.

'Will you come for a walk with me?'

Lil looked worried. 'Oh, I don't think so, I've got far too much to do.'

'What are you going to do?'

'The minister's coming. What time is it? I have to introduce him to the scriver.'

'Scriver?'

'You know, at the hall. You'll make me late.'

'But Lil it's Thursday. The minister comes and takes the service on Sunday, remember.'

'Not church, you silly girl. The minimum of yertle. Greens. Come on, we'll be late.'

Greens? Gabrielle thought of the woefully overcooked cabbage at the rest home. Surely not something to get back to so urgently.

'It's another hour till dinner time, Aunt Lil, we've got plenty of time for a walk.'

She got out of the car and walked round to open the passenger door. Lil allowed Gabrielle to help her to her feet but continued to grumble.

'I hope you know the way. There's only going to be one meeting here. I won't miss it, will I?'

Meeting. Greens. Gabrielle remembered Lil's passion for environmental politics. As they stepped on to the sand she said, 'Did you think there was a meeting of the Green Party today? I don't think there is.'

Lil stopped and faced her.

'For all your education you are not very understanding sometimes. I'm the guest speaker. Take me there at once.'

Gabrielle abandoned the idea of a walk on the beach and led her aunt back to the car. She sat with a beatific expression all the way back to the rest home and Gabrielle took her to her favourite chair in the lounge.

'Go now, I'm very busy,' said Lil.

Gabrielle remembered a day soon after Lil had settled into the rest home. She had told her niece a long rambling tale of how everyone had gone into the garden and had stood about waiting for some kind of entertainment. A circus, Lil had said, but nothing had eventuated and they had gone back inside.

'The nurses were very put out,' Lil said with some satisfaction. 'It was a very poor show. We waited around but the circus never came.'

Puzzled, Gabrielle had asked one of the staff if there had been anything planned.

'Oh, that was a fire drill,' said the young woman.

Lil's story was far more fun. Sometimes it seemed as if she was living in a completely different movie.

* * * * * *

In the small hours of the morning Gabrielle found herself listening into the darkness while she gathered her wits. That was definitely the sound of breaking glass. She lay very still, her heart jolting in her chest, her ears exploring the house. Another faint tinkle. Oh no, the counselling room.

Without turning on the light she picked up the phone from her bedside table and dialled emergency services.

'Police,' she said softly, then, 'I have an intruder.' She gave her address clearly, then she hung up and got out of bed. In the dark she found trousers and a sweater, put them on over her nightshirt and slipped her feet into shoes. She went quietly to the counselling room door and listened. A faint light came under the door and she could hear a rustling sound. She took a deep breath, thought of the self-defence instructor, and flung open the door shouting in a deep voice, 'What the hell do you think you're doing?'

A figure in a hooded jacket was bent over the desk with a torch. The head jerked up, startled, and the torch clattered to the floor as the intruder rushed at Gabrielle and pushed her hard in the chest. She landed painfully on her bottom, powerless to stop him as he ran out the open door and vanished into the dark garden.

When the police arrived five minutes later Gabrielle had put on the light but remembered not to touch anything. She showed the police the torch on the floor and the broken pane where the intruder had reached in to unlock the door. A number of files were on the desk, the top one open. Again there were no fingerprints and, in the garden, only one footprint in a flower bed by the gate, which had been hurdled at speed.

Gabrielle was proud of herself for not disturbing the evidence but the police told her off anyway.

'You should have stayed in your room till we came. It could have been dangerous. People have died confronting an intruder who was armed with as little as a bread and butter knife. What you did was very foolish.'

Her description of the intruder did not redeem her either. 'A dark-coloured hoodie, and jeans I think. I couldn't see any hair and I didn't get a look at his face. A bit taller than me.' It was too general to be much use. She couldn't even be sure that the individual was a male.

The key used to open the filing cabinet had been retrieved from its new hiding place under a vase.

It was almost dawn when the police left. Gabrielle sat on the steps, craving a cigarette even though she had given up a decade ago. Instead she breathed in the smells of the night-time garden and watched the sky turn from navy blue to grey. Just as a few clouds became pink-edged she looked down at her feet and began to giggle. She was wearing one black suede shoe and one sheepskin slipper.

Still a little hysterical, she went inside to check her office. There was no point trying to sleep at this stage, she may as well have an early breakfast and start the day. She would need a locksmith and a glazier to secure the room and her first client was due at 9.30. She straightened a chair, picked up the bigger pieces of glass, intending to return with the vacuum cleaner, and looked at the files.

All the Ls had been pulled out of their drawer in the cabinet and dumped on the desk.

Chapter Thirteen

Gabrielle ducked her head to enter the plane. In front of her, two Canadian girls were giggling nervously as they squeezed into their seats, one on either side of the aisle. No doubt it made a good story for their emails home: 'The plane was so small the pilot passed out the sweets on the way to the cockpit. And would you believe, I could see the co-pilot reading the map as we came in to land!'

The take-off was smooth and the plane turned in a graceful curve over Nelson as the sun was setting. Pink clouds decorated the sky and the lights below outlined the town against the bulk of the hills behind it. The plane turned towards those hills, rising sharply until there was only a cushion of cloud to be seen below and the darkening sky above. Nothing to do but settle down and relax for the half-hour journey.

Relaxing was not easy. Gabrielle had had a busy day and had rushed away after her last client. She was a little concerned at leaving the house unattended but the new deadbolts looked formidable and the glazier had used toughened glass to replace the broken pane in the door. The thought of meeting Martina again raised a more emphatic flutter of anxiety. Was she presuming too much? She had no way of knowing and Martina's 'give me a ring when you arrive' was enigmatic.

The plane touched down gently. That was a relief – the approach to Wellington could be rough and even seasoned travellers had been known to reach for their paper bags. Gabrielle had only a small carry-on bag so she walked straight through the airport, found a shuttle and was being welcomed into her favourite Bed and Breakfast place in Aro Valley in a very short time. She put her things into the 'Jungle Room', threw her jacket on to the zebra-striped bedspread and went down to the lounge to phone Martina.

'Come and have a drink with me.'

Gabrielle wrote down the directions and ignoring the fact that she had not eaten and that she could easily have walked to Martina's apartment in less than half an hour, rushed across town in a taxi. In the mall she found the flight of steps between the record shop and the Bangladeshi restaurant and went up to press the buzzer at the top. Martina opened the door and let her in with a hug and a smile.

'Wine? Brandy? Coffee?'

'Coffee thanks,' said Gabrielle as she took in her surroundings. The apartment was open-plan with polished wood floors and steel and glass furniture. A small kitchen was behind a counter and on the other side was a large dining-table with a tall glass vase of orchids on it. The leather sofa faced the uncurtained windows. Gabrielle sat down and became absorbed in the view of city lights and the dark hills beyond. If Nelson was a thin line, bravely held, Wellington was guerilla warfare, infiltrating the hills in every direction and showing its lights in unexpected valleys and ridges.

Martina brought coffee and a shot of brandy each and put the tray on a small glass table.

'You wouldn't need television,' said Gabrielle, indicating the view.

'I never tire of it, you know. It's different every day, all weathers. You can see the harbour from the bedroom and that's even nicer, especially in the morning.'

They sipped their coffee. Gabrielle became aware of jazz playing in the background.

'So what's this very urban lifestyle like?' she asked. 'What do you do when you're not working?'

'Go to the gym, meet friends for breakfast on the weekend. Shop. Maybe drive out to one of the beaches for coffee. Go to the Club some nights. What? Are you laughing at me? What do you do?'

'Quite boring really. Gardening. Walk on the beach. Go tramping with a friend some weekends. Go to the market on Saturday morning and get the week's vegetables and some plants for the garden. Now you're laughing.'

'It all sounds so wholesome. No vices?'

'It's way too small a town for vices, everyone knows what you're up to. What's the Club?'

'Abbi's. It's a lesbian nightclub. A friend of mine runs it.'

Gabrielle was aware that Martina was watching her reaction.

'Is it fun?'

The tension passed.

'On a good night. It's a buzz to see a crowd of women dancing, enjoying themselves. On a bad night I might be too aware of the dramas and bitchiness that go on. The young ones are a laugh – very out there and loads of style.'

'You're not a young one?'

Martina laughed. 'I feel young, but sadly no. Nothing like a bunch of out and proud 18 year olds to make you act your age.'

'Oh dear, I'm thirty-something, too.'

'Well, we're not quite in the over-fifties ballroom dancing category. You could come and have a look if you like. Tomorrow would be a good night, it's a rock and roll theme.'

Gabrielle smiled back at Martina's teasing expression. She had a sense a challenge was being issued.

'Love to,' she said.

Later, when the coffee and brandy were finished, Gabrielle rose and thanked Martina for her hospitality. She declined her offer to walk her back to her B&B and set out into the still-lively city. The air was cool on her hot face and she enjoyed covering the few down-town blocks on foot. Cafes were full and noisy conversation spilled out among the tables on the footpaths.

Two tall men, black-clad with dreads and piercings, met up with similarly styled friends and went into a bar. An older couple hurried by arm in arm. Gabrielle caught the woman saying to the man, 'I thought the third movement lacked cohesion but the cello solo was very moving.'

His reply was lost as they crossed the road.

Back in her hotel room she panicked. What on earth made her say yes to going to a lesbian nightclub? She had no idea how to behave or what to wear. There was something about the way Martina issued a challenge that made her want to prove herself, to take it up without flinching. She felt like a mouse running towards a cat.

* * * * * *

'"Lizzie Borden took an axe, gave her mother forty whacks,"' quoted Gabrielle to herself. She was in the University Library with a stack of journals and books to find out about women who kill their parents. How strange that anyone would think that rhyme was funny and yet many children fantasise about killing their parents and being left free to indulge in everything forbidden.

Actual murder of a parent, however, happened rarely and the researchers seemed to assume that the child who murdered their parent would be insane by definition. Gabrielle looked up Parker and Hume, two Christchurch teens who, in the 1950s, murdered the mother of one of them because they thought she was going to prevent them being together. They behaved so flippantly in court that, far from being considered insane, they got long sentences with no mitigation. And ironically ' it was a condition of their release that they never see each other again. ' As Gabrielle read on, she had a sense that even now the academics found it hard to explain what had occurred. She could not see any parallel with Jasmine.

After a morning of dense academic reading she did not feel much further ahead though she was convinced that a plea of insanity did not offer a very promising outcome for a young woman still in her teens.

It was a relief to leave the library and travel down by cable car to the shopping district. A brisk wind cleared her head and she turned her mind to finding a costume for the evening.

Fortunately, there was no shortage of second-hand shops and she soon found herself a flared skirt and a tight angora jersey. She also found a huge music shop and bought some CDs. She felt as if she had treasure in her bag. On the waterfront she bought falafel for lunch and watched the roller-bladers and the families in Flintstonesque pedal cars go by. Later, at a department store, she bought some hair ties and a pair of knee-length socks and felt reasonably confident she could do a rock and roll look. She picked up a Malaysian takeaway and went back to the B&B where she ate in the tiny kitchen and chatted to a middle-aged backpacker from Germany. It almost felt as if she was on her own travels.

Then she phoned Martina.

'What's the plan about the club?'

Martina sounded surprised. 'I wasn't sure whether it was the brandy talking. You really do want to come?'

'Of course. I've even bought a fifties costume.'

Martina laughed. 'I'd better dress up then. Shall I come to your B&B about nine? It's a short walk from there to the club.'

Gabrielle looked at her watch. Six o'clock. She wasn't sure how she'd fill in three nervous hours.

'Great. See you then .'

* * * * * *

'It's a bit weird isn't it?' Ethan was looking around the pink vinyl room.

'It's boring.' Jasmine made room for him on the bed and he sat looking miserably at her.

'We're in a mess, Jas. I gave Davey your clothes and the knife to get rid of and the egg just put them in my bin. The police got it all on day one.'

'They said.'

'And I went in to get your file but your shrink woke up and I had to run. I was scared she'd recognise me from when she came to see me. I've put her on to Spaz 'cause she's so keen to find out more. Pigs is really mad at her for getting all over everything.'

'God, Ethan, keep Pigs away from her, he's evil. She's only trying to help me.'

Ethan shook his head. 'I don't have any say. I don't reckon Pigs wants you helped, he wants you to go down for this.'

He got up, tried to pace the small room, then leaned on the wall.

'And Ram's not saying anything, the weasel. He's shit scared the cops will lock him up and throw away the key. So no one knows he's the one who found Don. Your shrink is so sure she was first on the scene. Feels responsible, eh?'

Jasmine was silent. Annoying as Gabrielle could be at times, she didn't want her to be hurt.

After a while she said, 'Don't s'pose you've got any stuff?'

Ethan stared at her as if she really was mad. 'Jeez, I thought they'd frisk me. Don't they give you anything? They have heaps of great stuff here for free – diazepam, rivotril, misties even.'

'Nah, it doesn't help. I want to get really wasted so I can forget.'

Ethan shook his head. 'Man, when this is all sorted I'm going straight. Go to Polytech like my Mum wanted and get a different life. This one's too weird.'

After a while he added, 'You know the worst part?'

Jasmine looked at him dully.

'I really did think I was going to be in a movie. There was the camera and the costumes – I liked the superman outfit best – and we could make up the stories. Even some of the sex stuff, I really thought it was acting like I'd seen on Shortland Street and Mum's soppy movies. I was so keen to be in the films, I thought it was really cool. Till he started hurting....' Ethan's voice trailed away. He stared hard at the floor as if his hopes lay in shards around his grubby trainers and, if he was really careful, he could still retrieve the pieces.

* * * * * *

Just before nine, the manager came to say that there was someone waiting in the lounge for her. Gabrielle took another look in the mirror, tweaked her pigtails higher and twirled her skirt. She wasn't sure about the bobby sox and rolled them down to her ankles, then ran down the stairs to meet Martina.

As she glanced around the lounge, she saw her dinner companion playing backgammon with another woman, and, standing by the window, a boy with slicked-back hair who was wearing a tight-fitting suit. He came towards her with a grin and for a moment Gabrielle was taken aback by his cheek. Then, like an optical illusion resolving, his face became Martina's. She flung open her jacket to reveal a narrow blue tie over a white shirt and she made a knock-kneed bow in imitation of Elvis.

'You look great!' Gabrielle told her.

'And you look just like Janet from the Rocky Horror Show,' replied Martina. 'Well done!' Again the boyish grin.

They linked arms and walked out into the Saturday night city. No one gave them a second glance.

'I could be dressed in a corset and fishnets and no one would even look,' said Gabrielle.

'Not at this time of night, darling, you might get some offers later on.'

Gabrielle punched Martina's arm lightly.

'Hey, that's not ladylike,' Martina protested.

They walked on till they came to a narrow doorway and some stairs. At the top of the stairs a shaven-headed young woman in a tux sat behind a small table with a cashbox on it. Martina handed over some notes. The music was loud: 'Stay away from run-around Sue...' Gabrielle was grinning already.

Inside, the dance floor was full of women. Some were in fifties clothes but not all. Gabrielle noticed that the pairings were quite random. Two women in full skirts and ponytails might be dancing together, or two in masculine outfits. Or any combination of skirts, trousers, fifties or modern. Some couples did a very good jive, others moshed. All looked as if they were having fun.

Martina said in her ear, 'The great thing about lesbians, they turn up and get into the mood right away. You don't have to hang around till midnight waiting for the party to get going.'

They worked their way around the edge of the dance floor towards the bar. This took some time, not only because it was crowded, but because Martina knew everyone and stopped often to introduce Gabrielle and exchange a few words. Finally they got a glass of wine each and found a small table where they could sit and watch the dancers.

A large woman with hennaed hair and a silk shirt came up to talk to Martina. Martina introduced Gabrielle and the woman shook her hand but seemed more interested in Martina. It was too noisy to have a three-way conversation anyway and Gabrielle continued to watch the dancing. One couple was particularly stylish, a slim woman in tight-fitting trousers and a white shirt, dancing with a more feminine-looking blonde in a green satin dress. They had all the moves of competition dancers and the green dress flared out as they twirled around each other. Other dancers near to the couple had stopped to watch and when the music ended and the couple finished with a flourish everyone clapped. Gabrielle did too, smiling broadly. The slim woman left the dance floor and walked briskly towards Gabrielle, veering to one side at the last minute to greet a woman standing behind their table.

Martina tapped her arm. 'Back in a moment.' She walked away with the hennaed woman still talking intently to her.

'Ok if I sit here?' Gabrielle looked up into the very blue eyes of the slim dancer.

'I haven't seen you here before. Are you new in town?'

'I'm from Nelson, just visiting. I'm Gabrielle,' and she held out her hand as others had done during the evening. The dancer shook it firmly.

'Jude. Do you dance?'

'Not like you, that looked professional.'

'Not really, just a passion of mine,' said Jude. 'I teach a dykes' ballroom and rock and roll class. Ange is one of my star pupils. We're going to take that routine to the Gay Games.'

'I didn't know they had dancing.' Actually Gabrielle didn't know anything about the Gay Games.

'Oh yes, it's not all running round on a hot field. Line-dancing, ballroom, rock and roll. All competitions. Then there are some great social events, the grand ball and a huge dance. It's good to have something a bit special for them.'

'Have you been to the Games before?' Gabrielle asked.

'I went to the last ones in Sydney with Roxy, but she dumped me while we were over there, it totally messed up our performance. You can't dance well together when you hate each other – it's more intimate than sex. I'm going to keep things strictly professional with Ange and have another go. I think we're in with a chance for a bronze at least – she's lighter on her feet than Roxy, anyway.'

The music had started again. It was too loud to continue the conversation but also Jude was instantly distracted, looking towards the dance floor and tapping her foot.

She held out her hand. 'Dance?'

Gabrielle took the outstretched hand. Jude pulled her towards the dance floor almost at a run and held her close. 'You'll have to teach me,' gasped Gabrielle.

'Just follow me,' said Jude and swung her round.

After a while Gabrielle found the rhythm. It was like rock-hopping: try not to think and let your body do it.

'Good stuff,' Jude called into her ear as she twirled her under her arm and spun her away, then with a twist rolled her up again like a yo-yo into a cross-armed hug. Gabrielle was flushed and laughing, concentrating on keeping up.

At the end of the music she thanked Jude and, mustering skills learned as a teenager, disengaged herself and went back to her table. Martina was sitting there without her friend.

'Jude didn't waste any time spotting new blood.' She didn't sound amused.

'She's an amazing dancer.'

'Oh yes. Such a pick-up line for her.'

Gabrielle laughed. 'Don't worry, she's just gone out for a smoke. I couldn't go home with a smoker.' She stopped, feeling awkward. She had just reassured Martina as if she was jealous. Was she? She glanced across the table and was relieved to see the ironic smile on Martina's face.

'Oh, so who would you go home with?'

Gabrielle hedged. 'I've hardly had a look around and only one dance. I'll have to tell you later.'

They watched a while longer. Then Martina nodded towards the dance floor with an eyebrow raised in invitation. Gabrielle smiled and stood up. No contact this time and nothing virtuoso, but Martina had a good sense of rhythm and the old 50s numbers were great to dance to. Gabrielle was enjoying herself. Martina gazed past her, either looking for someone or checking out the crowd.

The 'young ones' stood out. Startlingly white shirts, jeans and shaved heads were one uniform. Their round young faces under the bald heads unwittingly gave them the look of babies, though there was nothing babyish about the bulletproof air of confidence they gave off. Some were drinking beer from bottles, unimpeded by their numerous lip and tongue piercings.

Another style involved dreadlocks and layers of multicoloured fabrics. Piercings were part of this look too, mostly nose and eyebrows. Gabrielle pictured airport metal detectors struggling with these decorated young things.

'And that's just the piercings you can see!' she thought.

All kinds of styles seemed acceptable. An older woman with short grey hair and mannish trousers danced by with a young woman with a curly ponytail and brightly coloured harem pants. A Chinese woman leaned her sleek dark head on the shoulder of a round-bellied Maori woman whose springy curls curtained both their faces as she bent down for a kiss. There was a celebratory air in the room.

It was two in the morning when the music stopped, the lights came up and Abbi's started to empty. As they set off through the city streets, Gabrielle asked who the woman with the hennaed hair was and Martina replied, 'Ah, my ex, sort of. It's complicated. We haven't spoken in a while.'

'She looked kind of formidable,' said Gabrielle.

Martina laughed. 'You could say that.'

In return Gabrielle began to talk about Brenda. Martina stopped abruptly in front of a luridly painted Adult Shop and faced her.

'I wasn't too sure where you stood, you're kind of naive.'

'Brenda wasn't out, so we never had anything to do with the culture or the social scene. Then she went to Auckland and suddenly dumped me for a full-on lesbian feminist. It totally pulled the rug out from under my feet – I just hid away and licked my wounds, with only my brother and my friend Kathy to talk to about what I was going through. It's been a while now, but I lead a quiet life in Nelson and I haven't met anyone else.'

Martina looked at her thoughtfully. Then she grinned and arm-in-arm they walked on, talking animatedly about everything except the plain fact that they were going to Martina's place.

Chapter Fourteen

Martina poured two brandies and came over to sit beside Gabrielle on the sofa. She had taken off the jacket but still looked boyish in shirt and tie. Together they looked out at the changing neon signs and the headlights snaking below. Martina opened her arms and Gabrielle leaned against her. She was warm and soft, and smelled of something fresh, herbal. As Gabrielle turned to look at Martina, she met her kiss openeyed. It was completely absorbing and Gabrielle didn't want it to stop in case they had to talk about what was happening. Without breaking the connection between their mouths Martina slid down into the sofa, pulling Gabrielle on top of her and running her hand down her spine. Every vertebra became alert.

She nuzzled into Martina's neck and breathed in her perfume and the musky scent of her skin. She sighed. Martina murmured into her ear, 'Is this all right?' Gabrielle nodded. Martina slipped her hand under her skirt and gently massaged her thigh. Their second kiss seemed timeless. Martina broke away and said softly, 'We'd be more comfortable in the bedroom.' They got up slowly with their arms still around each other.

Martina turned back the duvet on the big double bed. Then she gently took the clips out of Gabrielle's hair and shook it out, stroking it with her fingers until it fell in waves around her face.

Gabrielle loosened Martina's tie and slipped it over her head. She undid the shirt buttons from top to bottom and pushed it down off her shoulders. Underneath, a singlet showed the shape of Martina's small firm breasts and the muscles of her upper arms. Her skin was golden with fine black hairs. The shirt fluttered to the floor with a sigh.

Martina sat Gabrielle on the edge of the bed and knelt to take off her shoes and socks. She massaged her feet and slid her fingers between the toes till a thrill ran through Gabrielle's body. Then she lifted the angora jersey over Gabrielle's head and dropped it on the floor. With a smile Gabrielle took off her own bra. She liked her round breasts and their strawberry pink nipples; she was happy for Martina to enjoy them as she knelt there between her legs and nuzzled and kissed them.

Then it was her turn to lift the slim-fitting singlet and caress Martina's breasts and their brown aureoles. She bent forward to take a nipple gently in her mouth and heard Martina murmur softly. She did the same for the other one. Standing up, she reached for the fastenings of her skirt but Matrina stopped her.

'Slowly,' she said.

Naked to the waist they hugged and kissed. Breasts and bellies caressed each other, hands and lips stroked and teased. Martina reached under the skirt and inched her hand beneath the knicker elastic. Gabrielle loosened Martina's belt and cupped both buttocks in her palms.

Locked in a deep kiss they slowly freed each other from the rest of their clothes. Breaking away, Martina put her hands on Gabrielle's shoulders and looked at her. They stood naked, face-to-face. Martina was taller and slimmer, her golden skin smooth in the soft lamplight. Gabrielle was pink-and-white and Rubenesque. Martina reached out to touch her light brown bush with a smile.

'You're beautiful,' she said and she led Gabrielle to the bed where they lay side by side stroking each other. A fine sweat made Gabrielle's skin shine and she arched her back to reach towards Martina's hand. Martina stroked the inside of her thighs then raked her nails down the soft skin, making Gabrielle gasp, not in pain but with pleasure. Martina's hand circled round and round, up one thigh, through the damp hair and down the other. Gabrielle's whole consciousness was filled with the movement of that hand. When Martina leaned forward and, still circling, took Gabrielle's nipple in her mouth, she cried out in surprise and delight. The circles grew faster, smaller and suddenly Martina plunged her fingers into the slick vagina which was aching to receive her. Gabrielle cried out again and bucked hard against the hand that she had been waiting for. They found their rhythm and worked together until Gabrielle came in shuddering gasps, gripping Martina's fingers with strong contractions. They found each others' mouths in a long deep kiss while Gabrielle's heart thudded audibly and she groaned as Martina withdrew her hand.

Gabrielle came back to herself and opened her eyes. Martina was smiling down at her. Gabrielle smiled back and rolled over so that Martina lay beneath her. She stroked the length of Martina's body gently once, twice, three times, then she took Martina's hands above her head, pinning the slim wrists with her left hand while her right stroked firmly – breasts, belly, pubic mound, displayed taut and open. She could hear Martina sigh as she gave herself up to the sensation without the need to respond. Gabrielle bent her head to lick the sweat from between Martina's breasts and slowly circled each nipple with her tongue. She knew Martina wanted her to take the nipple into her mouth but she too could make her lover wait. Still holding the wrists in surrender she teased with her tongue and brushed Martina's springy black bush with her hand. When she felt it rise to meet her she released her grip and inched down the bed, flicking her tongue over the flat belly. She slid down between the parted legs until she could see the wetness that was waiting for her, finding with her tongue the pearl which would make Martina cry out in her turn. When she felt Martina's rhythm begin to take over she slipped her fingers into the luscious wetness and joined her in the last deep beats which ended in an arching, bucking convulsion. As Martina's body slackened and relaxed Gabrielle moved back up to hold and kiss her and they looked deeply into each other's eyes.

'That was lovely, ' whispered Martina. 'How are you? More?'

'Maybe.'

This time Martina stroked her gently to a climax that flowed like water and let her float back down. When her heartbeat had settled she asked Martina, 'And you?'

Martina shook her head. 'I'm done. You're very good. You've been hiding your light under a bushel.'

Dreamily, they slipped under the covers, retrieved the pillows and fell asleep in each other's arms.

In no time at all the sun found its way over the ridge, across the harbour and into the apartment. A beam of light reached the pillow and warmed Gabrielle's cheek. She woke blushing as if from an erotic dream and saw Martina lying face down beside her. It was no dream.

She wriggled in to where she could lie along the length of Martina's body.

'Go away, you're insatiable,' mumbled Martina, while doing something which made it very unlikely Gabrielle would go anywhere. They snuggled together while the sunbeam moved off the bed and climbed the wall.

Suddenly Gabrielle had a thought.

'The B&B. I have to check out – what's the time?'

Martina propped herself up on one elbow and grinned at her.

'Ten o'clock. You'd better jump in the shower.'

'Come with me.'

She laughed. 'I don't think so. You'll be way quicker by yourself. I'll bring you a towel and some jeans – you can't go back in the Janet skirt. Now scram.'

Ten minutes later Gabrielle was walking down the road, her skirt in a plastic bag, her hair damp, wearing the angora jersey and Martina's jeans rolled up at the cuffs. In the shop windows she liked what she saw.

At the B&B she packed quickly, settled the bill and waited at the bakery for Martina to join her.

'I'll post the jeans back when I've washed them.'

'Keep them, they look good on you,' said Martina.

They ordered croissants and coffee and made them last. Gabrielle watched Martina's small brown hands dismember her croissant and thought of the pleasure those hands had given her. All too soon it was time to get a taxi to the airport.

Martina kissed her good-bye right there on Aro St for all to see.

Chapter Fifteen

'Hi Finn, is your Mum about?'

Since he had turned fifteen, Kathy's eldest son seemed to grow at an exhausting rate. This included his hair, which had become a tousled mop of brown curls hiding most of his face like camouflage.

He waved her through to the kitchen where Kathy was peeling a sink full of potatoes and ten-year-old Lucas was sitting at the table doing homework with his mother's complicity. As the youngest he had always tried to keep up with his brothers and lately this meant adopting a 'cool dude' image with beanie, wristbands and an oversize shirt with a number on it.

'Um, Holyoake, try that: H-o-l-...'

Gabrielle interrupted her friend with a hug which Kathy returned, stiff-armed, a potato in one hand and the peeler in the other.

'How's Mum's homework score?' Gabrielle asked Lucas.

'She's got this one wrong.'

Gabrielle looked. He was doing a crossword with the heading NZ History.

'The clue is "Prime Minister during the war. Something R – five letters.'

'Fraser?' she suggested.

'Cool, thanks Gabrielle.' He wrote it in. 'How about this one...'

'Hang on, I don't need the marks. I've come to talk to your Mum.'

He grinned at her and turned back to the crossword.

Kathy put the potatoes into a large pot and covered them with water.

'I can come back to these. It's like being in the army. I'll put the kettle on.'

'Can I help?'

'Lucas will do it, won't you Lu?'

'Only if you help me later.'

Kathy pushed his beanie over his eyes. She put the coffee in the plunger and set out two mugs and some milk on a tray.

'Bring it to the lounge when the water boils, fill it up to here, see?'

'What did your last slave die of?' said Lucas.

'He's in his room studying for a test, so you're it,' Kathy told him. 'And don't cheek your mother.'

Gabrielle hid her grin till they were in the lounge. 'He's full of beans.'

'Positive Parenting has a lot to answer for. He's got the jump on me now. I should have listened to my mother: "spare the rod and spoil the child"'.

'You wouldn't have it any other way. I can't imagine you scaring them, let alone hitting them.'

'Don't worry, it's been touch and go at times but I wasn't going to have them grow up the way we did, too terrified to say boo and no personality of our own.'

'I think you always had plenty of personality. The life and soul of Form Four as I recall.'

Kathy laughed. 'Something slipped through the cracks then, thank god for that. So how was your weekend?'

At that point Lucas came in slowly with the tray. He put it on a low table and gave an exaggerated bow. They thanked him.

'Do as much as you can of that crossword and I'll look at it later,' said Kathy. 'Dad might know some.'

As he left, Kathy turned to Gabrielle, 'So how was Wellington?' She looked as if she expected gossip.

Gabrielle stammered out something about shopping and the art galleries.

'I did do some research as well. I went to the University library and looked up some references Martina gave me about women who kill, especially when their parents are the victim. It's extremely rare. I don't know what the police are doing, going after Jasmine without looking at all the options. I have to find out more.'

Kathy held up her hands. 'Whoa! where's all this coming from? You helped her find a lawyer, there's an expert witness who can testify when the time comes. Why do you have to turn into a one-woman crusade all of a sudden?'

Gabrielle was hurt. 'I thought you'd be with me on this. You're usually the one who fights for justice. You thought I should get out into the real world. Well, this is the real world.'

'Honey, I certainly stand up for people's rights but I use the system, I don't try to do it all on my own. You have to follow the process.'

Gabrielle pictured Jasmine in the bare pink room. 'The process takes months. She won't stand months of solitary confinement. And she's totally vulnerable because she doesn't remember that night so she can be told she did it and she might believe it. The police need to know that there are other suspects out there. If I can just piece a bit of it together I can take it to Detective Parker and they can go from there.'

Kathy looked dubious, but Gabrielle was not to be put off.

'And then there's Ethan. Do you know who Ethan is?'

'Jasmine's friend-slash-boyfriend?'

'Well yes, but he was the ten year old kid who blew the whistle on Don Lawson. He told me himself. What if he felt threatened that Don was out of jail? We need to find out more about Ethan, and those druggy friends that were at court. And what was Ram doing looking for Jasmine so early in the morning?'

She looked at her watch. 'It's not too late to go and see Garth, is it? I need to find out what happened to Ram. I can't believe I haven't been back to see him, this last week has been so busy.'

Kathy took up that theme with a look of relief. 'I can help there. Talia said he's doing all right. He'll be in hospital for quite a while longer, his leg was badly broken and he had to have surgery to pin and set it, but she said he was sitting up playing a Gameboy when she visited. In my experience that usually makes a young man cheerful.'

'Hmm.' Gabrielle was not about to open her plans to another protest from her friend, but it wasn't an update on Ram's broken leg that she was after. She quietened herself, drank her coffee and turned the conversation to Kathy's boys, a distraction so familiar to Kathy she didn't notice she was being diverted. One of the spin-offs of being a counsellor, thought Gabrielle. By the time she left, Kathy almost certainly thought her friend had calmed down and seen sense.

Round at Garth's, Talia opened the door with Ruben in her arms.

'I seem to keep turning up at bedtime and I miss out on playing with my favourite people,' said Gabrielle, thinking of a similar scene at Toby's place. Ruben, bathed and pyjamaed and clutching his bottle, was not inclined to socialise. Talia called Garth, who offered Gabrielle a seat at the kitchen table and put the kettle on.

They made small talk about the week, the weather, and Garth's work as a bouncer in town, till Gabrielle worked her way round to Ram. Another news bulletin about his health added little to what Kathy had said but then Gabrielle broached the subject of his friends.

'It must be lonely for him in hospital. Who did he hang out with?' she asked.

'He didn't bring any mates home. I think he had friends at the English School, they might see him right. They sent cards and stuff.' Garth grinned. 'He liked a bit of weed. Cultural, you know, his people grow the stuff quite openly. He found some mates to smoke with but I doubt they'd be the hospital visiting type.'

'Do you know who they were?'

'Hardly stuff we talked about. The missus is totally against it. I didn't even tell him where to go when he asked how to score, but he said he found out ok.'

'What about girls?'

'He'd flash himself up and go out at night smelling of aftershave, like a Romeo. He was definitely keen on someone, but I never saw her. I told him when he moved in he's to live his life, we weren't going to police him.'

Talia came back from putting Ruben to bed, made herself a drink and sat at the table with them. They talked a bit more about Ram, then about Ruben's birthday party which was shaping up to be quite a family gathering.

Eventually, Gabrielle made her excuses and left. She was still curious about Ram and why he was so afraid of the police. Maybe she could see him at the hospital: there was nearly half an hour before visiting hours finished at eight thirty.

As Gabrielle parked she noticed how tall the trees had grown around the perimeter. She had hardly ever been to the hospital at night and the walk from the carpark to the main entrance seemed eerie.

The enquiries counter was closed for the night and so was the gift shop, but Gabrielle knew the way. In Ward 8 the lights were dimmed and a sole nurse sat at the desk. Gabrielle asked after Ram and was directed to a different room from the one he was first in.

'He was having nightmares and keeping the other patients awake so we've given him a single room,' the nurse explained.

The room was at the end of the corridor. Through the open doors of the side rooms Gabrielle could see that some patients had visitors still sitting round their beds, others were already settled down for the night. At the door of the end room Gabrielle paused, doubting she was in the right place. Someone with long blonde hair was bent over the bed as if kissing the occupant. She knocked and said, 'Excuse me...'

The blonde straightened abruptly, then rushed out the door, knocking Gabrielle aside. As she stared after the figure which barged through the double doors to the lift bay, she realised it was a man, not a woman, and there was something familiar about him. Her brain searched for a match but she was brought sharply back to the room by the sound of coughing from the bed. Ram was trying to sit up, pushing a pillow on to the floor and struggling for breath.

Two quick steps took her across the room to his bedside and she slipped her arm under him to raise his shoulders. At the same time she reached for the bell and held her thumb down on it.

In the few seconds it took for the nurse to arrive Ram had regained his breath. He shook his head at the nurse.

'Ok now, just choke,' he said, coughing a little to demonstrate.

'There was a man here...' Gabrielle began, but Ram interrupted.

'Wrong room, gone now.' He lay back, drained.

The nurse picked the pillow up off the floor and straightened the bed. She made sure that Ram was comfortable and could reach his water jug.

'Five minutes,' she said to Gabrielle, before returning to her desk.

Gabrielle sat by the bed. 'Ram, what's going on. Tell me.'

He shook his head. He was still a little blue around the lips and his breath rasped in his throat but he insisted there was no problem.

'Ram, I saw him. He was doing something to you.' She tried to make sense of the brief image she had. 'He had that pillow over your face.'

Ram's face crumpled. 'Bad man, wants I say nothing. So...' he gestured with his hand as if wiping something away. 'Nothing to say.'

Before Gabrielle could work out how to persuade him to say what was happening, there was a soft flurry in the corridor. The other visitors were making their way to the lifts, the nurse gently shepherding them out.

'Ram, I have to go. But talk to Garth, he knows how to handle these guys. Promise me you'll tell Garth what's going on. Trust him, he can look after you.'

She looked hard into the brown eyes of the little man on the bed. He looked back and she could see fear and then something else. Acceptance. He nodded. She patted his hand and followed the last of the visitors out to the lift. As she got into the car she heard a motorbike roar off into the night.

It was after nine by the time Gabrielle reached home and carried her weekend bag inside. Suddenly she was dead tired and she wished she had come straight home from the airport instead of playing detective. She had learned nothing and gained only confusion.

The phone rang and, as she picked it up, her heart lifted in the hope that it might be Martina.

She said softly, 'Gabrielle here.'

There was silence.

'Gabrielle here.'

Silence.

'Hello?'

A sharp click as the caller hung up. She pulled a face at the phone as she put it down.

She had just poured a wine when it rang again. Silence then click.

By the third call Gabrielle was frightened and angry. She wished she had a whistle to blast the caller's eardrum. Instead, she said forcefully into the silence, 'If you do this again I'll get the call traced.'

A hoarse voice said, 'We're watching you, bitch. Keep your nose out of things you don't understand.'

Gabrielle slammed the phone down as if it had bitten her.

Chapter Sixteen

All through Monday morning Gabrielle felt jumpy and out of sorts. After her first two clients she sat down to write their notes. It was hard to focus and all too often she found herself staring blankly out of the window.

From the corner of her eye, she saw a movement in the hedge. Not the flutter of the blackbird, something slower, more furtive. As she watched, the top of a dark head appeared.

Going quickly to the kitchen, she slipped out the back door. The watcher was fixed on the front of the house, unaware that a side gate would let Gabrielle into the street behind him. Opening the gate softly, she could see the back of a slim figure in a black hoodie.

From two metres away she said in a calm voice, 'So what's going on? You're stalking me.'

He wheeled round. Was it the same person she had seen the night of the burglary? He seemed smaller and less menacing, a pale, wide-eyed boy in his early teens. With relief she noticed that his hands were empty – there was no weapon.

She raised her own hands, palms open. 'Don't panic. Just tell me what's going on.'

He glanced up the street assessing whether to run for it, then back at her. She waited, holding eye contact. His pupils were so dilated with fright his eyes were black. He drew a long breath as if he was about to speak – and burst into tears.

Gabrielle stepped forward and took him by the arm.

'Come inside and tell me about it.'

She led him through the little gate and into the kitchen where she handed him a paper towel and a glass of water and sat down at the table with him.

'What's your name?'

'Simon.'

'I'm Gabrielle. Ok, Simon, I think you've been peering through my windows, you've broken into my house and now you're watching me. You didn't steal anything when you had the chance but you've been tampering with confidential files. I could just hand you over to the police but I'll give you a chance to explain yourself. What's going on?'

His eyes, still teary, were very dark and frightened.

'I...' his voice collapsed in a squeak. He coughed and started again on a deeper note. 'I haven't broken in, I swear. I was just watching your place.'

'Why?'

'I'm adopted. Mum and Dad didn't tell me when I was a kid, they saved it up to hit me with on my fourteenth birthday. I'd never guessed, though when they told me it kind of made sense. I don't look like them or my sister and I don't like the same things. But then lots of kids don't like what their parents like.'

He stopped. To calm him and keep him talking, Gabrielle asked conversationally, 'What kind of things do you like?'

'Music. I play bass in a rock band. My family's very sporty, they're always off to netball and soccer and stuff. Dad coaches soccer and Mum still plays netball.' He clearly thought she should have grown out of it. 'My sister's a cycling rep. She bikes for hours all weekend. I never saw the point.'

'So it made sense when they told you that you were adopted. What else did they tell you?'

'That after my sister Mum couldn't have any more kids. That I can't look for my real parents till I'm 18. But I got my birth certificate out of Dad's file and found out their names.'

'So how come you're spying on me?'

'I looked them up in the electoral roll. My mother's name wasn't there but my father lives around here. I staked out his house and followed him here one day. I thought he might be meeting my mother. I looked at your mail so I knew you weren't my mother. Then I saw you're a counsellor and I thought I better find out more. My father might be psycho or something.'

'People don't come to see me because they're psycho.' Gabrielle couldn't resist putting him straight. 'They come because they need to talk things through. But you can't just invade people's privacy like that.'

'What else can I do? I have to wait four years otherwise.'

'Maybe I can help but you have to cut out the private eye stuff and do it the proper way.'

He nodded.

'What are their names?'

'Helen O'Connor and Peter Goulding.'

That backed up his story that he had not rifled her filing system – the Os and the Gs had not been touched.

'Are you sure you've got the right person?'

Simon looked at her as if she was stupid.

'When I saw him I was sure. He's small and dark like me. I just knew.'

'Ok. Well, I'm going to get you a pen and paper so that you can write Peter Goulding a note. Next time he comes I'll explain that you got in touch with me hoping to meet your birth father. Put in the note how he can contact you if he wants to. Then it will be up to him.'

She got up but Simon put out a hand.

'He can't phone me at home. Mum and Dad don't know I'm doing this. Couldn't I just come back here and find out what happened? And I want to know what he's like, can't you tell me something?'

Gabrielle felt uncomfortable. There were rules for this kind of thing and, really, Simon's adoptive parents should know what was going on. The simplest solution would be to hand Simon over to the police – let them work out whether he was the intruder – but the lad looked so earnest and sad.

'I can't tell you anything about him, that would breach confidentiality. But he's not psycho.'

She put the pen and paper on the table in front of Simon.

'Write your letter and I'll give it to Peter next time he comes. What happens next is up to him and your parents.'

Simon nodded unhappily. He reached out his left hand to pick up the pen and began his letter. He covered the first page in a dense scrawl and flipped over to the next. And the next. On the fourth page he stopped, wrote 'Simon' and underlined it, tore off the sheets and, folding them neatly, handed them to Gabrielle. She was touched that he had so much to say.

Gabrielle put the letter into the envelope and sealed it.

'Anything else?'

He shook his head. He looked exhausted. She resisted putting her arms around him.

'OK, that's it then. No more stalking.' She opened the back door. 'Just one thing. Why the threatening phone call?'

Simon looked at her in surprise. 'I haven't ever phoned you. And why would I be threatening? I want you to help me.' He shook his head. 'It wasn't me.'

* * * * * *

Gabrielle had a full day booked and she kept busy until the evening. At last she was able to pour a glass of wine and sit down in her favourite chair with Copland's 'Appalachian Spring' on the CD player. She tried to think over what she knew about Don's death. She sketched out a time line but nothing seemed to add up. She wrote 'suspects' in capitals and put Jasmine's name underneath, then Ethan and after a moment's thought, Ram. Then below that 'the caller'. In case there was someone completely unknown as yet, she added 'X' . The list didn't seem to help much. In detective novels they look for motive, means and opportunity, but almost anyone could have the first two, hatred for a paedophile was such a widespread feeling and knives were everywhere. Opportunity? Not many people, including the police who were trying to keep tabs on him, knew that Don was in Nelson, let alone at Jasmine's flat. That brought her back to the obvious answer, the one she didn't want – Jasmine.

She picked up the phone and dialled Martina's number, relieved to find her at home.

'Martina, it's been a weird re-entry after such a marvellous weekend. And I've been getting crank calls. I wish you were here, I could do with a crime-busting buddy – and a hug.'

Was that a slight pause?

Then Martina said, 'Actually I do have to come to Nelson to talk to Freda and to interview Jasmine.'

'You're welcome to stay here. I'd like to show you my house.'

Another pause. 'I'll see what flights I can get. Maybe tomorrow night?'

'I'd really like that. Tomorrow then.'

As Gabrielle hung up, the miasma of unease returned. It would be lovely to see Martina again but she had sounded a bit reluctant just then on the phone. Gabrielle had a disorienting sense that nothing was quite as it seemed, that she could not trust her own judgement – about the murder or about where she stood with Martina.

Her head spun and she realised she was too tired to think about it any more. She turned up the music as 'Spring' reached out in a glory of faith. 'Nice for Copland', she thought and she set about cooking herself a meal.

* * * * * *

The next day, feeling guilty about her duplicitous visit on Sunday night, Gabrielle bought Kathy lunch in town. Over strong coffee and paninis filled with delicious mushrooms and mozzarella, she told her friend a more truthful version of the weekend in Wellington.

Kathy was thrilled for her. 'Honey, that's great. It's been so long since you and Brenda split up, you deserve some happiness.'

Gabrielle gave a wry grin. 'Happiness? That's a tall order and it's early days. But I must say it was exciting to be close to someone again.

It's as if a whole dimension of me has been asleep for years. It definitely brings the senses alive.'

'Makes the world go round,' grinned Kathy. 'So tell me. What's she like?'

'You can see for yourself. She's coming to stay the night, her flight gets in about seven and she's booked to leave on the last flight out tomorrow. Come round after work tomorrow and we'll all go for a walk together.'

Kathy nodded. 'Done.'

They ordered another coffee each and while they waited for it to come, Gabrielle said, thoughtfully, 'What do you think of adoption?'

'If only I'd thought of it sooner,' said Kathy. 'No one would have them now.'

'Silly. I mean in general.'

Kathy raised an eyebrow. 'More "strictest confidence"?' she asked.

'Sort of. I can't really give you the whole story but it turns out my stalker was a teenager looking for his birth parents. He thought I could help.'

'Can you?'

'I can. But should I?'

'I can't imagine not knowing. Everyone needs to know who their people are and where they come from.' Kathy grinned. 'Better to know that your people drive you nuts than to die wondering.'

'I guess I need to give it some thought. I want to help the boy but his adoptive parents have their rights, too. It's complex, I shouldn't go blundering in.' Gabrielle fell silent. She could take the matter to Rona that afternoon. Surely she would have some advice.

Kathy broke the silence. 'At least that solves the stalker problem. That's a relief.'

To reassure her friend, Gabrielle nodded and tried to look pleased. She did not want to mention the phone call or let slip that she had not given up on her sleuthing. As she left the restaurant, she felt that Kathy's enthusiastic thanks for the lunch were undeserved – she was still being dishonest with her friend.

* * * * * *

Rona, when asked about the adoption issue, gave a typically 'on the one hand, and on the other' answer which left Gabrielle to face the issue herself. So she moved on to Martina, the weekend in Wellington and how thrilled she was that this exciting woman was coming to stay the night. She even admitted to the note of hesitation she had discerned in Martina's voice on the phone.

Rona thought for a moment.

'Let me tell something. When my Tama died I thought my life had ended too. I wanted to lie down beside him and never get up. Sure, we had our fights. Tama tackled everything head on. He'd yell and shout, stomp off and come back still glowering. I'd wait, think of a way round things and when the moment was right I'd make him laugh. I could always make him laugh.

'When he knew he had cancer we talked about where he would be buried. I wanted him near me but the right place was in the family urupa with his parents and sister and all the old ones. In the end we came up with an idea. We bought a kowhai tree and planted it together out the back here. By then he was so weak he had to sit in a chair and watch me dig the hole. Still bossy though, he made me dig it deep and put in lots of compost. Then he held the tree while I filled up the hole and he put in the last few spadefulls. When I stamped it down he said, "Make sure you plant me good like that," but he wouldn't let me cry about it. "I've had a good life," he said.

'It's done well that tree. In the spring it's covered in golden flowers and full of birds. When I want to talk to Tama I go out and talk to that tree.'

Rona paused.

'The day Tama died I looked out the kitchen window and there was Piwaiwaka the fantail, flitting round Tama's tree. She's the messenger from the other side. I said, "Go away, I don't want your message," but it was time. Tama died that afternoon and he was ready to go. My sisters came and we took him up North to his home marae. We carried the coffin into the Meeting House and I sat beside him for three days and nights, hardly eating or sleeping. People came and went, spoke to me, spoke to him. Told him off for leaving us all too early, for leaving me.

'We'd been together since we were young things in the hostels in Wellington. We'd work all day in the factory and at night he'd press his trousers and put on a fresh white shirt and I'd put on my best dress and we'd go dancing or partying with the other young Maori who had come to the city to work. We'd come home in the small hours of the morning and he'd climb in my hostel window and make love till the sun came up. Then we'd get up and go to work and do it all again the next night.

'When we moved here he did up this house for me and I was the gofer and helped him with the painting. He's all around me now.'

Rona smiled, remembering. She looked at Gabrielle. 'I'm telling you all this because Tama was my true mate. I've been alone these ten years but I don't regret it. I was lucky to have him and I don't want anyone else. You have to find your true mate. It wasn't your first girlfriend and maybe it's not this Martina. But if you find your true mate, you'll feel blessed. '

As Gabrielle was leaving, Rona took her through the kitchen to the back door and together they looked at the kowhai tree. There were no golden flowers in this season, only feathery leaves and seed pods which hung down like stiff tight beans. They were about to go when they saw a black and white shape fluttering in the branches.

'See,' said Rona, 'The fantail has come from the other side to tell me that Tama is thinking of me.' There were tears in her eyes.

Chapter Seventeen

Gabrielle whistled a little tune as she backed down the drive. She grabbed a flier that was poking out of the letter box and dropped it on the passenger seat.

Typically, the plane was delayed. Gabrielle paced around, pretending to look at the art on the walls. At last the announcement came and the plane landed. Martina was one of the first to come across the tarmac, striding through the glass doors with a small sports bag in her hand.

Gabrielle hugged her. 'Is that all your luggage?'

Martina grinned. 'Travelling light. It's only one night.'

As she got into the car, Martina picked up the piece of paper from the seat. 'Is this a joke?'

Gabrielle glanced at it. 'Some flier or something. It was in the letterbox as I was leaving home. What does it say?'

'I think you'd better look for yourself.'

The thick black letters said 'We're watching you.' Red felt pen made blood drops down the page.

'Oh god.' She put it in her handbag, trying to look cool – surely criminologists were threatened all the time. 'I'll give it to the police tomorrow,' she said, thinking, 'I'm glad I won't be alone tonight.'

Martina looked concerned but said nothing.

They drove back around the waterfront, past the restaurant where they had had dinner the first time they met and where they had walked, looking at the sea and telling their stories. Waves broke on the rock wall, sending up a fine spray. The sky had darkened to navy blue and the street lights made orange patches on the water.

Gabrielle showed Martina around her home, including the room where she worked. She was proud of the place she had created for herself and pleased with Martina's response.

'So cute and cottagey. It's exactly the kind of house I imagined you in!'

'I'll show you the garden in the morning. Not that there's much to see at this time of the year but I'm still fond of it.'

They settled in the living room with a glass of wine each. Gabrielle went over what she knew so far.

Martina was reluctant to go into it. 'All the people you've mentioned seem to be connected with Jasmine, though, don't they? I'll talk to Freda tomorrow and she can take up whatever she thinks will help. And since I'll be interviewing Jasmine later on, I'll see for myself what she's about. Enough shop for now?'

Gabrielle nodded. 'I know, I'm a bit obsessed; I could talk all night about it. I guess it's just work to you but everything about this situation is new to me.'

'It's not "just" work, I enjoy applying what I know to an actual case, but it is work and we could talk about other things.'

Gabrielle laughed and topped up their glasses. 'What other things would that be then?'

She got up from her chair and sat beside Martina on the sofa. Taking her glass out of her hand she put it on the table and leaned across to kiss her gently on the lips. She ran her hand through the short black hair which felt soft to her touch and drew Martina closer as their kiss deepened. She could feel the muscles of the other woman's back and the bones of her shoulder blades through the jersey she wore. The downy feel of the wool was very sensual. The floral-and-musk perfume of Martina's skin was familiar now and Gabrielle breathed it in and sighed.

Forehead to forehead they looked into each other's eyes. Gabrielle thought how lovely brown eyes are, before sinking wordlessly into another kiss.

Martina pulled away first. They were both half-kneeling on the sofa, face to face. Martina slowly withdrew her hand from Gabrielle's blouse and Gabrielle, suddenly shy, buried her face in the wool-clad shoulder. Martina pulled way further and looked into her face.

'This doesn't feel right.'

'It feels perfect to me.'

'We're colleagues, on a case together.'

'Does that make a difference?'

'It does to me.'

Gabrielle sighed and got up, straightening her clothes and fastening her buttons. To cover her embarrassment she went into the kitchen and put the kettle on.

Martina followed her. 'I didn't mean to hurt you...'

'I feel a fool, I misread the situation.'

'Not entirely, you are very attractive.'

'Tea?'

'Do you have any brandy?'

'No, but how would that help?'

'Ok, tea then.'

Gabrielle made up a tray and carried it through to the lounge. Martina sat on the sofa and Gabrielle sat in her armchair.

'So how has Wellington been ...'

'What have you been up to besides this case ...'

They both spoke at the same time, then broke off.

'What's wrong with this picture?' Gabrielle thought.

Later, lying in bed alone, she wondered if Martina already found her boring and she wished she could find a way to impress her. Then tiredness overcame her and she fell into a deep blank sleep.

* * * * * *

The morning began well enough with coffee, breakfast and a quick tour of the garden in the autumn sunshine. They had a laugh over the now-recovered gerbera and how the stalker had turned out to be a troubled kid. As Martina left in a taxi for her appointment with

Freda, Gabrielle offered to cook dinner for them both and take Martina to the airport. Martina accepted with a smile and a light pat on her shoulder.

Encouraged by this little gesture, Gabrielle went into her therapy room to look at her day's bookings. She nodded with satisfaction as she looked at her diary. There was a gap in the afternoon which could give her time to find Spaz and be back before Martina returned.

Her clients did not appear to notice that she was pre-occupied.

At four o'clock she wrote a note for Martina, and set off for Washington Valley with a knot in her stomach. She was not sure what Ethan meant about Spaz being the 'least worst' of the group but she told herself she would just be asking for help and if there was any sign of trouble she would apologise and beat a retreat. She parked in front of the big old house Ethan had described and walked up the steps to the sleep-out. The curtains were drawn. She jumped when her knock set off a loud barking inside.

A male voice cursed the dogs into silence and then yelled, 'Who is it? Piss off, I'm asleep.'

Gabrielle called back, 'I want to talk to you about Jasmine Lawson.'

There was a silence, then the door opened. A stocky ginger-haired man stood there in a dirty t-shirt and shorts. Two dogs crowded in behind him, growling.

'Are you a cop?'

'No, I'm Jasmine's counsellor. I'm trying to help her.'

He jerked his head towards the interior of the room. Gabrielle hesitated to pass the two evil-looking dogs, one short and thick-set with a pit-bull look about him, the other a tall black Doberman whose curled lips seemed startlingly close to her face. Spaz cursed them back and they slunk under a table where they settled uneasily into a nest of grubby blankets.

Gabrielle stepped over the threshold and sat gingerly on the one vinyl chair. Beside her a table was covered in pizza boxes and take-away containers. A bottle of milk had separated into yoghurty lumps floating on urine-coloured whey.

Spaz shut the door and took a couple of jerky steps across the room to collapse heavily on the bed. There were no sheets on the stained mattress and the blankets were indistinguishable from the dogs' ones.

'Well?' he snapped.

Gabrielle realised she had been holding her breath, partly in fear and partly as a defence against the foul odours of dog, unwashed man and decaying food.

She took a breath and began to explain.

'You know Jasmine?'

He nodded.

'She's in the Mental Health Unit, the police think she killed her father.'

'Nothing new so far.'

'The night Don died you were with Jasmine and some others at Ethan's flat.'

'Who says?'

'I've talked to her,' said Gabrielle. Suddenly it didn't seem a good idea to mention what Ethan had said or the fact that Jasmine had no memory of that night.

'So?'

'What happened that night? Can you tell me about it?'

'What makes you think I was there?' he hedged.

'You were there. So what happened?'

'We had a few beers, bit of a laugh. Nothing wrong with that.' He looked at the floor, then glanced up slyly to see how she was taking his evasions.

'Who else was there?'

'D'ya think I'm some kind of nark? Waddaya getting at?'

At his raised voice the short dog stood up and the Doberman lifted its head. The room felt very small to Gabrielle as she sat between the wary dogs and the defensive man.

She controlled her anxiety and said calmly, 'Not at all, there's nothing to hide is there? Just a few beers with friends. Jasmine needs your support, it might help if you and some of the others speak up and say she was with you.'

'Speak up to who? The cops? That'd be the bloody day.' He spat on the floor in disgust.

'Tell me a bit more about what Jasmine was doing at the flat.'

'Trying to get out of it same as the rest of us. Drinking our booze and smoking our dak like all the free-loading bitches. Wouldn't put out for it either. She slapped me and started screaming. Bloody Ethan took her side, fancies his chances but I know she's just a ball-breaking bitch. He called me a fucking cripple. Bastard. Then he went into the bedroom with her to try it on. Fat chance, she's frigid. She's a bitch, why should I help her.'

He was shouting from the bed and both dogs were on their feet now, growling. Gabrielle sat very still and spoke softly, even though her heart was almost deafening her.

'I see what you mean. You must have been pissed off with both of them. Did they stay in the bedroom or come back to where the rest of you were?'

'They come back. Ethan calmed her down, he can always get round the chicks. He brought her back 'cause Davey had some P and we were all going to get into it. So we had to share it with the bitch cos she said it would calm her down.'

'Then what happened?'

'She started talking. What a downer! On and on about her sad life – jeez. I'd've left but I got a ride with Pigs and it's too far to walk back to town. Even the P didn't make it better. On and on she went, my old man this, my old man that. Jeez, whose old man wasn't a fucking bastard? Ethan and Davey all sorry for her. Then Pigs started on his sad story. What a fucking waste of P! In the end I walked anyway just to get away from the whining.'

'Who are Davey and Pigs? Where would I find them?'

Gabrielle jumped in fright as Spaz leapt to his feet.

'Two-faced bitch, you just want me to nark on my mates don't you? Wheedle it out of me then go off laughing like all the bitches.'

By now both dogs were barking in her face. She tried to stand but Spaz pushed her down on the chair and the dogs became more frenzied. She could smell their hot breath, the barking made her dizzy. Her heart was racing as she struggled to breathe.

Pulling on a pair of jeans, Spaz pushed his feet into dirty trainers, muttering under his breath.

'Get the Boss. The Boss'll deal with her ...'

The dogs quietened and stood growling, looking from Gabrielle to Spaz. Perhaps they hoped they would get out for a walk.

He said, 'Stay! Guard!' and they lay in front of her, watching her closely. The Doberman twitched his ears towards Spaz as he opened the door, and gave a little whine, but Spaz said again, 'Guard!' and went out. Gabrielle heard the key turn in the lock.

The two dogs lay, poised to spring, between Gabrielle and the door. She wistfully pictured her cell-phone on the seat of her car as she took stock of the room. Even the movement of her head made the dogs look up, alert. In the boredom of their daily lives this task was a novelty and they intended to do it well.

She was facing the door which she had heard Spaz lock, the two dogs crouched side by side at her feet. To her left, less than an arm's length away, was the table. A good step to her right, the bed was a nest of matted blankets and stained pillows and at the foot of the bed, on the same wall as the door, tattered curtains partly hid the window.

She looked at the dogs. The short one growled but the Doberman twitched his ears towards her. Perhaps he was not entirely hostile. She thought of her father's farm dogs, tough working beasts which were by no means pets, yet even they craved a pat and a kind word.

Patting was out of the question if she wanted to keep her hand. She took a few slow breaths to calm herself and spoke softly.

'Well, old fellas, this is going to get a bit boring. Bet you haven't even had breakfast yet, eh?'

They were definitely listening.

Gabrielle scanned the room again. Food would be helpful. The table was covered in scraps but the dogs would gulp pizza crusts in a second. The takeaway containers might divert them a bit longer as they licked out the residue of chicken marsala and rogan josh.

Moving slowly and keeping up a soothing patter Gabrielle reached out for the nearest container and lowered it to the floor just under the edge of the table. Shortie remained staunch but the Doberman checked it out. A tentative sniff proved satisfactory and he settled down to lick the plastic clean, still with one eye on Gabrielle.

It took him all of thirty seconds to dispose of the curry. There were two more containers and some pizza remains. That would buy a minute and a half at the most – not very helpful.

Beside her, almost behind her head, was a set of shelves fastened to the wall. Still babbling gentle nonsense she turned to study them. There were dusty plates and cups, a packet of teabags, a leaking bag of sugar and ... a huge box of dog biscuits.

'Party time, fellas. Just let me stand up and get these and we'll all be happy. What do you think? Din-dins?'

The babyish word seemed to find recognition in their canine brains. Both dogs pricked up their ears and the Doberman positively grinned. Moving like a busker pretending to be a statue, Gabrielle rose from the chair and grasped the box in her left hand. It was heavy, a good sign.

She dropped a biscuit beside each muzzle. Even Shortie had his price. The room filled with the sound of gnawing and crunching.

Dropping another two biscuits each and murmuring endearments, Gabrielle moved to the bed and knelt on the mattress behind the piled bedding. She pulled aside the greasy curtain with one finger; the window had a very ordinary catch which would be no trouble to open.

Facing the dogs, she threw a few more biscuits. Their ears twitched as the window-latch clicked but they kept on crunching.

The window jammed.

Gabrielle pulled one of the pillows towards her, then opening the box wider she bent forward and poured all the dog-biscuits on to the floor. As the dogs fell on this bonanza, Gabrielle leaned heavily on the window. It burst open and she thrust her head and shoulders awkwardly through.

Shortie leaped on to the bed barking ferociously. She stuffed the pillow into his jaws and he seized it and shook it like a rat.

Gabrielle fell out on to the path and scrambled up to slam the window shut before Shortie could jump after her. The two dogs set up a terrifying racket but Gabrielle felt high on adrenalin and success.

She turned to run down the path and collided with a vast man. He wrapped his arms around her like an embrace.

'That's her, Garth,' said Spaz as he limped up the path.

Chapter Eighteen

After the psychologist had gone, Jasmine lay in a tight curl on the plinth bed. There was a distant moaning which she gradually realised was herself. She curled tighter, wrapping her arms around her knees and making herself as small as possible. She squeezed hard as if she was squeezing the images out of her brain. For a few blessed moments all she could see was blackness, but then the pictures flooded back in: Don laughing; Don turning to pull out a chair and sit down at the table as if he was never going to leave. He folded his arms and his laughter grew louder and louder, his body grew bigger and bigger until he was a giant and she was an insignificant little rabbit, staring at him with stunned round eyes. He would do what he liked, he always had. She might squeak out ' no ' but he wouldn't hear it, or wouldn't care. She squeezed her knees harder, trying to make him go away.

She noticed the dressings on her wrists. In the last few days the bandages had been replaced with sterile pads. She picked at one. The sticky edge curled up and came away from the soft skin of her arm with a slight burn. Good. The burn was good. Don receded and Jasmine put all her attention to getting the tape off. She tried pulling it quickly, like your mother pulls off sticking plaster, but that shortened the pain. With all her concentration she pulled slowly, savouring the burn which filled her brain with a pure light. Slowly, slowly, the pad came away. She stared at the bristly black sutures. The skin was beginning to seal in a puckered pink seam. She plucked at one knot. The pain was sharper. From far away, almost floating, Jasmine watched herself bite through the black thread. She pulled it out and a flower of blood opened at the end of the wound. She had cut vertically up the vein, only silly girls who don't really mean it cut cross-wise. As she bit into the second stitch she could taste the salt-and-iron of her own blood. Blood was good, blood made pure. The second stitch fell on to the blanket. Jasmine drifted, rocking slightly. She could no longer feel the pain, only the purity. This was where she wanted to be.

An alarm rang out and running feet pounded down the corridor. The door of her cell banged open and someone was shaking her, smacking her lightly on the cheek, and lifting her into sitting position while someone else raised her arm above her head, hurting her but not in a good way. She looked down at the bed and when she saw the blanket soaked in blood she started to scream. She screamed and screamed until more running feet brought the needle that sent her off to oblivion.

* * * * * *

Spaz unlocked the sleep-out while Garth steered Gabrielle firmly up the steps and back inside.

The dogs leapt and barked. Spaz shook his head at the remains of the box of dog biscuits on the floor.

'Jeez,' he said, 'those aren't cheap.'

Garth pushed Gabrielle down on the bed. She looked at her friend with a worried frown. Why was he treating her like this? He shook his head very slightly and his right eyelid fluttered in the shadow of a wink. She tried not to look relieved.

'Get those fucking dogs out of here,' Garth snapped at Spaz. Spaz caught a collar in each hand and dragged the dogs outside where he chained them up.

'And shut them up for God's sake.'

Spaz threw a handful of the biscuits at them and slammed the door. He stood in front of it, arms folded, on guard.

Garth sat on the chair Gabrielle had so recently vacated and looked at Spaz. 'Piss off will you, I want to talk to the lady alone.'

'It's my place,' Spaz began with a whine, then stopped when he saw Garth's expression. 'I'd go and get a pie or something but I'm broke, eh.'

Garth fished in his pocket and threw a $5 note at him.

Spaz cringed at Garth, 'Mate, we're staunch, aren't we?

Garth sighed. 'Spaz, I'm not your mate.'

Spaz started to say something, thought better of it and disappeared.

As the door shut behind him for the second time Gabrielle turned to Garth with a relieved smile. He did not smile back.

'For crying out loud, Gabe, what are you doing with this low-life?'

Gabrielle tried to explain but it sounded feeble now. What had she been trying to prove? Besides she had questions of her own.

'Why did he call you Boss?'

Garth frowned. 'History. I'm not happy that he came and got me, I have to say. I've made a clean start with Talia and Ruben, I don't need pond scum like Spaz thinking I'll be there for him in his time of need. Let's get out of here before he comes back.'

Before they could make their move, the dogs started barking again and there were raised voices outside. Garth opened the door. Spaz was stamping about on the path, shouting and shadow-boxing.

'More of the bitches. Piss off, I'm not having an open home. Jeez, leave a fella in peace would you.'

Gabrielle peered under Garth's arm. At the end of the path Martina and Kathy were gesticulating and trying to reason with Spaz who looked like Rumplestiltskin having a tantrum.

'Spaz!' said Garth. He hardly raised his voice but it penetrated the cacophony.

'Shut it.' The dogs and Spaz fell silent. Garth turned to Gabrielle. 'Friends of yours?' She nodded. 'We're all going to have a little chat.'

She looked in awe at this street-boss version of Garth.

To Spaz he snapped, 'Go back to sleep and forget anyone was here. Especially me. Got it?'

Spaz protested, 'But I didn't get me pie yet ...'

Garth gestured to the sleep-out. 'Get!'

Spaz went inside and shut the door without looking back. Gabrielle followed Garth and he gestured for Kathy and Martina to go with them.

They fell in without argument and walked in silence down the road to a little park. They sat around a picnic table. Gabrielle waited for someone to speak, noting with embarrassment that her friends were not happy with her.

Garth began. 'I've said my piece, I'm not going to have anything rocking my boat. Don't link me up with low-life again.'

'I'm sorry, Garth, I had no idea he'd get you involved...' Gabrielle began.

Kathy jumped in. 'What were you thinking? I said leave it to the police, you're not V.I. Warshawski. In the real world we let the experts get on with the job. I was worried sick when I realised where you'd gone.'

'How did you even know? How come you two turned up together like that?'

'Did you forget? We were all going to go for a walk.' said Kathy.

Gabrielle blushed. She had forgotten completely.

Kathy went on. 'I turned up and found Martina pacing the floor with your note in her hand. "Gone to see Spaz, back soon" wasn't much to go on but we ransacked your desk and found the bit of paper with the address. You must tidy up sometime, girl, but today it was a good thing that you keep everything. Including Carol's card, by the way, my next move would have been to call her.'

She was flushed with anger and worry, as if one of her boys had gone missing.

Gabrielle groaned. 'Thank god you didn't. It's bad enough having all my friends angry with me without the police knowing I'm playing private eye.'

She turned to Martina and could hardly meet her eye. 'I guess you're angry too.'

'You have to leave it, Gabrielle. Freda's building a very good defence and she's a competent lawyer. I interviewed Jasmine this afternoon and we can really help her. But if you're going to be a loose cannon, it could all come to nothing. If you care about Jasmine, just step back and let the legal process take its course.'

Gabrielle studied the planks in the table. She'd failed in both her objectives: she had not found anything new that could help Jasmine, and Martina was certainly not impressed. Her investigations looked amateur and foolish under the scrutiny of three people whose opinions she valued. She felt like crying.

Garth put his hand on her shoulder. 'Don't look so down, Gabe, we're still mates. Just stay out of it, ok?'

She nodded.

He held out his hand across the table to Martina. 'Pleased to meet you, I'm Garth.'

Martina shook his hand. 'Martina.'

Pleasantries dealt with, Garth got up. 'Better get back before the whole village lets Talia know I'm down in the park with three lovely ladies.'

He turned to Gabrielle. 'I went and saw Ram yesterday. He seems to have got himself mixed up with those drug-dealing scum, Spaz's mates. They've been threatening him, but he reckoned it was sorted. I said to tell me if there was any more trouble and I'll see them off.'

He nodded his good-byes and strolled off down the street.

It was growing cold and Gabrielle noticed that the sun had gone below the brow of the hill. It must be getting late.

'Oh my goodness,' she said to Martina. 'Your flight! If we make a run for it we might still get there in time...'

Martina shook her head. 'Don't worry. I decided this afternoon that I'd need a bit longer. I've changed the flight. If that's ok with you?'

Kathy stood up and brushed down her skirt. 'Time for me to get back too. Why don't you come and have dinner at my place? I'd like to get to know Martina better and find out what really did happen in Wellington.'

'Kathy!' Gabrielle's cheeks grew even hotter. But Martina had already accepted.

Nothing more was said about the incident during the rough and tumble that was family dinner at Kathy's place. Martina seemed to fit in just fine. The boys, after an initial shyness, showed off for her by bickering and topping each other's stories and Jim, clearly delighted to see Gabrielle 'with' someone, made himself the charming host.

When the boys had finished squabbling over the dishes and had gone to their rooms to do homework or play hip hop music – or both, as they maintained – and the adults had settled in the lounge with brandy and coffee, Gabrielle felt forgiven. She began to tell Kathy and Jim a little about going to the nightclub in Wellington.

Kathy was enthusiastic. 'Why don't we go somewhere? Girls' night out.' She looked at Jim who grinned and nodded 'sure'.

'But there isn't a women's club here and besides surely no one goes out on a Wednesday,' said Gabrielle. She felt awkward about going out again with Martina, in the light of the confusion of the previous night. On the other hand, maybe it would be just the atmosphere they needed.

'There is a nightclub run by women, it's called "Trixie's" – I hear all the time about what fun it is. Can you stay tomorrow night, Martina? Thursday must be a good night to go out.'

Martina suggested including Freda. 'I could get an early flight back on Friday morning and go straight to work. Why not?'

As they left Kathy's place Gabrielle began to dread going back home with Martina. She made a detour past Toby's house and , seeing lights on, suggested they call in.

'It was Toby that suggested I contact you in the first place. He did your workshop a while ago.'

'The pathologist, right?'

Gabrielle nodded.

Martina gave her a warning look. 'We're not going to talk about the case, are we? I've read his report, there's nothing I need to discuss with him, especially not informally. And you're off the case, right?'

Gabrielle sighed. 'I know. I just want a nightcap with my brother and you'd enjoy meeting him. He's a nice guy.'

Chapter Nineteen

'You know that sever woman?' said Lil, as Gabrielle manoeuvred her into her jacket.

Gabrielle looked puzzled.

'S-e-v-e-r, the sever woman. She's someone's mother, or maybe daughter.'

'Which one is someone's daughter?' asked Gabrielle.

'No, grandmother,' said Lil.

Gabrielle abandoned any attempt to follow. She knelt down to re-tie one of Lil's sturdy brogues.

'Let's go out,' she said.

They began a circuit of the garden, and Lil said, 'Reesy.'

'Yes, it is breezy. Quite a cold wind in fact,' said Gabrielle.

Lil looked amused. 'I said "reesy".'

They were lost again. As Gabrielle helped Lil up some steps and into the small rose garden, she seized the initiative.

'I went tramping the other weekend. Not the best weather for it, we got soaked in fact, but I did enjoy getting out into the hills. Do you remember going up to the cave? We did that together one summer. The cave was a disappointment, though, very small and you couldn't really go into it. I thought it was going to be a proper cave, one with stalactites and stalagmites.'

'Stalactites, hold on tight. Stalagmites, you might fall over,' quoted Aunt Lil.

'Well done! I remember that one. Good for you,' said Gabrielle, impressed that the mnemonic had somehow surfaced among Lil's tangled neurons.

'You sound surprised,' grumbled Lil, 'it's not anything brilliant.'

'Do you know some more?' asked Gabrielle. 'How about this one: "Sticks and stones..."?'

'... will break your bones, break your mother's back and marry a rat,' finished Lil.

'That would be pretty bad, wouldn't it?' Gabrielle smiled and was rewarded by a glimpse of her aunt's famous wry humour as their eyes met. But the light soon flickered out. They trudged on around the flower beds.

Gabrielle was doggedly sticking to her routine, accepting that she was 'off the case' as Martina had put it. She had given Martina free run of the house and, while she saw her clients in her counselling room, Martina set herself up with laptop and cell-phone at the kitchen table. On her way to visit Lil, she had dropped Martina at the Mental Health Unit to see Jasmine for another interview, on the understanding that Martina would find her own way back. She felt a pang. Not only did she hate being out of the loop and not knowing how the assessment was progressing, she also felt bad that it was some time since she had visited Jasmine herself.

Even calling in on Toby had been uneventful. He had put the kettle on and they talked softly in the kitchen over mugs of hot chocolate. Crystal was already in bed and, of course, it was far too late for Gabrielle to show Martina her beloved niece. But Toby was as affable as ever and although they didn't talk about 'the case', he and Martina had professional stories to swap, including some school-boyish attempts on Toby's part to gross out his audience. Martina proved equal to anything he could throw at her, even coming back with some of her own, from her days in the forensic unit at the prison. Her description of her own welcome ceremony, when she was a fresh young psychologist, made Toby and Gabrielle laugh. She had had to hongi the inmates, some of the country's worst murderers, as part of the Maori-style welcome. Pressing noses and eyeballing these huge, 'criminally insane' men had been an awe-inspiring induction into the job.

As they left, Toby had given Gabrielle a hug and whispered, 'She's cute,' in her ear. She had rolled her eyes at him and he had raised an eyebrow. How come everyone but Martina thought they were a great match?

They completed a round of the rose garden and Gabrielle took Lil's hand to see if she was warm enough. Lil curled her chilly fingers around Gabrielle's as trustingly as a child. Touched by the innocence of the gesture, Gabrielle held her hand all the way back to the lounge. She helped Lil out of her jacket and kissed her on the cheek, then left her aunt talking in tongues to the woman in the next chair, who talked back with a monologue which was unaffected by feedback in any language. They seemed happy enough, thought Gabrielle, as she hung the jacket in Lil's wardrobe and said good-bye to the nurse on her way out.

Once in her car, she checked her cell-phone. There was a text from Martina. 'Come to MHU ' – bit peremptory if she was asking for a ride home. But far from being irritated, Gabrielle felt her spirits lift as she turned away from the sea and drove towards the Unit.

Martina was in the office, talking to the young doctor, Philippa, when Gabrielle arrived. The doctor opened the door for her and she stood in front of the two women, noting their expectant expressions.

'Are you ready to come home?' she asked Martina.

'What? Oh, no, that's not why I called you,' said Martina. She looked to Philippa to explain.

'Jasmine had a set-back yesterday after Martina interviewed her. She removed her sutures and by the time the nurse did her routine check, Jasmine had lost a lot of blood. She got hysterical at the sight of the blood-soaked blanket and we had to sedate her. We're not keen to have Martina continue the assessment unless we can be sure Jasmine can cope with it. Unfortunately she's not talking to any of us, so Martina had the thought that you might be able to get through to her since you've known her the longest.'

Gabrielle looked at Martina with raised eyebrows. What did this mean in terms of her 'off the case' status?

Martina understood the implied query. 'Can you just find out how she is and whether she can stand up to seeing me again? I'd really like to finish my assessment.' In professional mode she was polite and rather distant.

Gabrielle followed the nurse, Penny, down the corridor to the now familiar secure area.

'Personally,' said Penny, 'if it's a criminal matter I reckon she should be in the Forensic Unit in Christchurch. We're here to treat mental health issues, we're not jailers or lawyers. All this interference from outsiders just makes our work harder.'

Gabrielle considered herself on notice: she was not to upset the patient.

Penny unlocked the door. 'Jasmine, your counsellor's here.' She waved Gabrielle inside and locked the door behind her. Gabrielle glanced at the buzzer with a slight feeling of panic. Her way out.

She sat at the foot of the bed where Jasmine lay huddled as before. She started talking softly about how she had been thinking of the young woman and wondering how she was getting on, how pleased she was to be able to visit. There was no sign that Jasmine heard her. Tentatively she put her hand on the bump at the end of the cotton blanket which was Jasmine's foot. It was not unlike talking to Lil, one-sided and with hardly a clue as to how the message was getting through. She thought of Lil's fingers curled trustingly in her own, and patted the small foot in the hope that some contact would be reassuring.

'You're having a very rough time just now. I can understand how you might want everyone to go away and leave you alone but we really do want to help you. I tried to find out more from Ram but he's still in hospital with his broken leg and he didn't seem to want to talk.'

Gabrielle had the feeling that Jasmine was listening to this. Was there a slight change in her breathing?

'Ethan put me on to this guy Spaz, so I went to see him, but he wasn't any help either. He has these evil dogs, and they bailed me up, but I got away ok.'

Jasmine mumbled something and Gabrielle leaned closer to hear her.

'You went to see Spaz?' The young woman sounded incredulous.

'I hoped he might be able to help you.'

Jasmine gave a grunt that was almost a laugh. 'Him? He can't even help himself.'

'So I saw,' agreed Gabrielle. 'I haven't been able to be much use, I'm afraid.'

Jasmine pushed the blanket away from her face and glanced at Gabrielle. 'Thanks for trying. No one can help. They should have let me die.'

Gabrielle drew a deep breath. At least they were talking.

'There seem to be an awful lot of pieces of the puzzle missing. Maybe if all the pieces were on the table Martina or your lawyer might see something that can help you.'

'The University professor from Wellington?' Jasmine snorted. 'Why can't I just talk to you?'

'You can.'

Gabrielle held her breath. This was not what she was supposed to do but if it was what Jasmine wanted…

Slowly Jasmine sat up and wrapped her arms around her knees. She gave Gabrielle a sharp look through her hair, then concentrated on the new bandages on her wrists.

She began to talk.

Gabrielle listened intently. When Jasmine came to the end of what she had to say and was calm again, Gabrielle asked her if she would tell all that to Martina.

Jasmine shook her head.

Or even see Martina one last time?

Jasmine was dubious. Gabrielle explained that the psychologist needed to finish her assessment and would fly back to Wellington in the morning.

'The nurses are afraid you'll get upset again, so they want to be sure you can handle one more interview.'

This seemed to touch Jasmine's pride. Of course, she was staunch enough to handle a shrink.

Gabrielle pressed the buzzer and while they were waiting for the nurse to release her, Jasmine grabbed her hand. 'Don't tell anyone what I told you, will you? I'll tell the shrink the important bits.'

Reluctantly, Gabrielle agreed.

* * * * * *

Later, as she cut up vegetables for a casserole, Gabrielle thought about what Jasmine had said: how she had opened the door to her father and instantly felt six years old again and completely in his power. When she realised that he wanted to stay with her, she had mustered all her assertiveness to say no. She remembered him sitting down at the table as if he was mocking her attempts to stand up to him and was making himself at home. As she ran to Ethan's for help, she thought of him laughing at her, the way he had when she was a child, when he held her out at arm's length while she flailed helplessly at him and his laughter filled her small brain with hot rage. Only while she had been alone in the secure unit had it come back to her that when Don sat down at the table he was not laughing. He sat as if the wind had been knocked out of him, he had looked frightened and he had said, 'Please honey. They'll kill me.'

She had left him there and run to Ethan. Crying, she had told Ethan that Don had turned up and she needed to get rid of him. Ethan had listened, looking stunned himself, and when his mates arrived they had asked her to tell the story again. They had offered her weed and P 'to help her get over the shock' and then they had all gone back to her place, assuring her they would get Don to leave. She could barely walk, she was so high, but instead of fearing her father she was full of fierce bravado.

When Gabrielle had asked her what had happened next, Jasmine had begun to hyperventilate. It had taken some time to calm her down.

Jasmine didn't know what had happened. She could only remember holding a knife and staring at a pool of blood on the floor.

'I must have killed him,' she had whispered, 'but I don't remember it. Now all I remember is his frightened face, and how he needed me to help him.'

As Gabrielle stood at the bench, tears ran down her cheeks. Jasmine would surely confess to murder and there was nothing she could do about it. There was an odd parallel with Lil: neither woman, young or old, could tell the truth because the truth was locked up in a brain which would not yield it. It made them equally vulnerable.

Chapter Twenty

By nine o'clock Gabrielle, Kathy, Martina and Freda were in Kathy's room, giggling like a bunch of teenagers. Liberated from her lawyer's uniform, Freda was colourful in a purple silk top and dark gold trousers which took up the colours of her cherry and auburn streaked hair.

Gabrielle wore her little black dress which didn't get out much these days. She had put up her hair but Kathy teased out a few wispy bits and redid her eyeliner. Martina had a black velvet bomber jacket and tight jeans.

Kathy, with her flying cloud of red hair and a strappy layered burgundy dress, looked ready for anything.

'You'll freeze!' Freda said to Gabrielle as they folded themselves into Kathy's VW.

'I don't want to lose a jacket. I'll be fine when we get there,' she said.

It was nearly 10 when they arrived at the door of the club. The music was blaring but the dance floor was empty apart from a baby-faced couple who appeared to be holding each other up as they slow-danced in defiance of the tempo. The DJ looked as if he was saving himself for later. A few patrons, mainly male, were propping up the bar and a middle-aged man with a comb-over was chatting to the barman.

Kathy glared at the dancers. 'I should send them home. No way are they eighteen, I know that girl's mother. And it's a school night.'

Gabrielle gave them a worried look but Freda laughed. 'Settle down, they're not our business.'

The four women stood out like exotic birds in the bare room. They chose a table and Martina went to the bar for the first round. She came back with a handful of glasses and bottles of pre-mixed drinks.

They made their choices and Kathy and Gabrielle poured the lurid drinks into their glasses. Martina drank hers from the bottle and Freda went to the bar for mineral water.

Gradually more punters began to arrive. The youngsters left the floor and sat in a corner holding hands. Gabrielle wondered if they would have a curfew. A loud group of six or seven arrived and immediately began to dance.

Kathy looked around. 'I feel like Rip van Winkel. So this is what people have been doing while I got married and had kids.'

Martina nodded to Freda and they went out on the floor together. Gabrielle, envying the way that Freda looked au fait with it all, wished that she had had the first dance with Martina.

She leaned close to Kathy and said in her ear, 'How come Freda's so at home here?'

Kathy laughed. 'I think she goes up to those gay clubs in Wellington. Shall we join them?'

Gradually the club filled up. As it got busier they took turns to stay at the table and look after their things. Around midnight it was Gabrielle's turn. Kathy inevitably met someone she knew and was dancing as if making up for her lost youth. Martina and Freda had evolved a salsa-style dance which they were clearly enjoying together. Gabrielle watched, feeling side-lined.

The young couple were making their way to the door, still symbiotically entwined. She'd been right about the curfew – it was pumpkin time. The middle-aged man was still propping up the bar. His carefully combed lock of hair had slipped from his bald patch and was dangling behind his ear. He leered at a young woman whose top just covered her breasts, leaving her midriff and shoulders bare. While Gabrielle was watching, the man reached out and patted the young woman's behind. She slapped his hand away and shouted something at him. Impossible to hear but not hard to guess what. The man was mugging 'can't you take a joke?' when a young man built like a heavyweight boxer loomed up. Mr Hands shrivelled like a used condom. The heavyweight put an arm around his girl's bare shoulders and they took their drinks to a table across the room.

The dance floor was a seething mass. The DJ had come alive and was spinning and jiving at his turntables. Lights flashed from red to blue to green with an occasional searchlight beam splitting the room and dazzling the eyes.

It took a moment to realise that someone was talking to her. A tall man in his thirties was smiling down at her and indicating the chair beside her. She nodded. It might distract her from watching Martina and Freda.

'Roger,' he said holding out his hand. They had to lean close to hear each other.

She shook his hand. 'Gabrielle.'

They smiled and nodded. Anything more detailed was drowned by the music.

'Drink?' Roger mimed.

Gabrielle spoke in his ear. 'My friends will get a round soon, but I'd love a juice.' She named a brand of apple juice that came in individual cartons.

Roger nodded. He left and she could see him at the bar. His height gave him an advantage and he returned quite quickly with two boxes of orange juice.

'No apple,' he mouthed and she took it, with a smile to say 'Thank you.'

Gabrielle peeled off the straw and used it to pierce the little silver circle that would let her in. This was always tricky. Either the tip of the straw bent and wouldn't pierce the foil, or it went through at a rush and squirted juice over your clothes. She was relieved to achieve entry without mishap. She looked up. Roger was sipping his and grinning at her. She mimed 'phew' and he laughed. He had a nice face, tanned and kind of boy-next-door, his hair was short and well cut and he wore a stylish jacket.

'Are you from out of town?' she yelled in his ear.

'Business trip. From Auckland,' he answered. She shrank a little from his warm breath on her ear. They watched the dancers and sipped their drinks.

* * * * * *

As Gabrielle washed her hands, the sound of the water running seemed far away and oddly distorted. Her face in the mirror was purplish and blotchy and her eyelids felt like blinds with broken springs. She forced herself to keep them open but really she just wanted to lie down on the floor. When she went to the door on spongy legs she found Roger waiting on the other side. He smiled and took her arm.

'You look a bit the worse for wear. How about a coffee?'

Gabrielle wanted to say she should go back to her friends, but the room looked too vast to cross and she could not form any words. It was easier just to nod.

Roger's grip was firm and reassuring. She made it to the door, where Roger said good-night to the bouncer as if he was a great friend. Gabrielle looked at the stairs and felt a distant flicker of panic. She glanced at Roger.

'No problem,' he said, 'I've got you. Hang on to the rail.'

They went down one step at a time. Gabrielle thought of that phrase and started to giggle about how she used it with clients and how true it was, but she couldn't be bothered explaining it to Roger. He held her in his powerful hands while they waited for some people to come up the stairs and Gabrielle closed her eyes for a moment. Her knees seemed connected to her eyelids and they folded too.

'Hey, hey, not yet, let's just get to the taxi,' said Roger. One of the men going into the club winked as he passed.

It was a great relief that a taxi was parked right outside, almost opposite the stairs. Gabrielle vaguely thought there was something she should do but the upholstery welcomed her in as Roger got in beside her. She tried to tell him her address but her tongue had grown thick and lazy so she leaned her head back and closed her eyes. When Roger spoke to the driver, she felt glad that someone else was in control.

As Roger helped her out of the taxi, she tried to say how kind he was to look after her but could only make a sort of gargle. He seemed to understand and nodded and smiled at her. He half carried her to the door, propped her up while he reached into his pocket for the key, then pushed her inside. Collapsed on the sofa in a wave of gratitude that she could at last lie down, she was irritated by a vague sense of alarm, like an oven timer ringing in the back of her brain. What was she supposed to do here?

A toilet flushed nearby and Gabrielle raised her head to look around the room. It looked familiar, but fogged like an old photograph. There was a word for the place but it buzzed at the edge of her brain just out of reach. The sofa she half lay on, the TV, a bench with a kettle and a small cupboard, a dining table and chairs all added up to something. Ah yes, a motel, that was the word: she was in a motel.

Roger came out of the bathroom. He had taken off his jacket and unbuttoned his shirt and underneath he was wearing a white singlet. Gabrielle wanted to giggle, it looked old-fashioned and silly. Wife-beaters, some people called them. He had zipped up his trousers but had not done up his belt and he was pulling it out of the loops. The oven timer was more insistent and an instinct leapt up in Gabrielle so that, though she still could not find words for the situation, she knew she wanted to run. In her mind she leapt up and raced out the door and down the path. In reality, she sat up limply and tried to force her rubbery legs to obey.

'Got to go,' she said. It was slurred but at least it was English. Roger put the belt on the sofa beside her. He nodded towards the door he had come through.

'Toilet? Again?'

She nodded. He sighed and helped her up. She leaned on the door jamb and waved him away.

'Private,' she managed and he stood back to let her through on her own.

'Well don't be long,' he said with a crooked smile.

She shut the door and leaned against it, willing herself to think. Slowly, as all her movements were slow now, she slid the lock across.

She looked at the shiny white sink and remembered the hand-basin at the club where she had felt really ill and Roger had rescued her. She struggled to recall why she had been there in the first place. A voice in the back of her head insisted that this was important. It was something about Kathy – and Freda – and dancing with Freda, Martina.

Yes – the girls' night out at Trixie's.

Roger rapped on the door. 'Come out of there.' His tone was sharp and irritable.

'Just a minute,' she whispered. It dawned on her that this was no rescue, she had been abducted. Adrenalin kicked in, beginning to clear the fog in her brain and as she shook herself awake, something landed beside her with a soft thud. Her bag had slipped off her shoulder where it had clung through the whole process.

'In the bag,' insisted the voice in her head.

She opened it and saw a wallet, some tissues and ...

'Phone.' The voice was guiding her now. She looked closely at the phone and was about to dial when she thought of Roger on the other side of the door. She crawled over and flushed the toilet. Then she spoke quickly and softly into the phone, 'Police. I'm in a motel. I'm sick and there's a man...' she tailed off, realising as the officer on the other end asked which motel, that she had no idea where she was. Taking a wild punt she said, 'Friends at Trixie's. Help me.'

The cistern had quietened to a soft hiss. Roger knocked again on the door.

'Come on out now, don't go to sleep on the floor, there's a nice soft bed here and I've made the coffee.'

Gabrielle put down the phone and looked at the door. It seemed strong and the lock was stout. Beside the basin was a rail with two thick white towels. They looked deliciously cosy.

'Ok,' she called to Roger as she pulled the towels down on to the floor, and, putting one under her head and one over her shoulders, curled up in the foetal position to let her tired brain switch off.

It was like torture. No sooner had she allowed herself to drift than Roger was banging on the door shouting at her to open it. She pushed her back against the door even though the blows he struck made her head ring and juddered all through her body. She still kept dozing off in spite of the noise.

Then the banging was further away and a shrill woman's voice chided, 'This is a single unit, if you bring someone else here you have to pay extra. And quit that noise, the neighbours are complaining.'

Gabrielle was about to emerge and throw herself on the woman's mercy, but the door banged and sharp footsteps receded down the path. Discouraged, she sat down again on the floor. She was chilled, her thin dress and the towel around her shoulders no match for the autumn night.

Soon there was another, softer knock and the sound of low male voices. Eager not to miss her second chance, Gabrielle opened the door.

'Help me,' croaked Gabrielle. Three men stared at her. She was kneeling in the bathroom doorway, unable to trust her drug-rubbery legs to stand. With one hand she held on to the door jamb, the other clutched her handbag.

'Excellent,' said Roger. 'Get her in the car.'

As the two men in the doorway stepped forward out of the dark night, Gabrielle got a shock that squeezed the breath out of her. These were not rescuers. The eerie fluorescent glare of the motel living-room caught the long pale hair of one of them, as they grasped an arm each and hoisted her to her feet. Her only possible resistance was to stay limp but they anticipated that and swiftly lifted her off the floor, carrying her by her elbows and half-throwing her into the back seat of a car which was parked in front of the motel door. The long-haired man got in with her. Roger and the other man shut the front doors and they pulled way, tyres crunching on the gravel drive and then drumming on the smooth surface of the road as they gained speed.

Chapter Twenty-One

Through heavy eyes, Gabrielle studied the man beside her as he sat look-ing out the half-open window. His blond hair reached the shoulders of a faded denim jacket, his black jeans had frayed patches on the thighs and his leather work boots were worn through at the toes to expose the steel caps. She searched her memory for a match. In the cold night air her mind was clearing even though her limbs still felt heavy and it came to her that he was the man who had left Ram's hospital room in a hurry; his face as he had pushed past her that night was as clear as a Polaroid. But where else had she seen him? Ah yes, when Jasmine was charged, he was at court with the man in motor-bike leathers and they rode off on the motor-bike together. Checking the man in the driver's seat, she recognised the jacket and his greasy smell. Kathy had said they were trouble.

She found she was still gripping her handbag and surreptitiously she slipped the strap over her shoulder, bandolier-style.

The rhythm of the tyres changed and they bumped over pot-holes; from time to time a branch scraped the panels. So, they were in forest, not far from town. The car braked, then the engine was cut and as the front doors slammed, Gabrielle made a quick decision to play possum. It wasn't hard, she felt like roadkill.

Roger spoke first. His voice was no longer engaging and seductive. 'Well, there you go. Do it.'

The man beside her was not happy. 'Here? You can still see the street lights. I thought we agreed to do it in the forest.'

'Shut up, Pigs, this is forest. See, trees. Plenty goes on here that no one ever knows about, you don't have to go completely bush.' This was the third man.

Roger snapped at him, 'You, Davey, get digging.'

The leather-clad man went to the back and opened the boot. There was a scrape of metal on metal as he pulled out some tools.

'I thought...' Pigs began.

'That's your job,' Davey told him quickly, 'since you're the great bloody hunter.'

Roger spoke sharply. 'Get on with it. GHB doesn't last forever.'

Pigs was not happy with the division of labour. 'I did my share back in town. I don't see why we got another job.'

'You took the money quick enough, don't start arguing now. We had it all set up just fine till this nosy bleeding heart got involved. The girl was convinced she'd offed her old man while she was out of it on P. You did a good job there. But no, this bloody woman has to start proving otherwise.'

'The girl still might plead guilty.'

Davey spoke up. 'Don't be a wally. Do you want to go to jail for the rest of your natural? Just get on with it, like the man says.'

He stepped away and began to dig, grunting with each shovel-full. Gabrielle started to shake – he was digging her grave.

Roger leaned into the car and grabbed her arms. She could smell his sickly aftershave and she tried not to gag. He pulled her upright so that she was standing on the pine needles.

She flung her arms around Roger's neck. 'Darling, why are we here? You had a nice bed for me.'

She attempted a clumsy kiss on his cheek.

He pushed her hard against the car. 'Don't fancy yourself. You're about twenty years too old for me.'

'But I'm only thirty-six,' she said.

He snorted. 'Make that thirty years too old. Pigs, get on with it, she's getting lively.'

Pigs looked at her and Gabrielle held his eyes for a long moment. He was younger than she had expected and his eyes were hazel, surprisingly clear in the headlights of the car. He looked frightened. Staying very still, she kept her eyes on his face. Maybe the drugs were wearing off for Pigs too, and with it the bravado.

'Shit, man, I don't know ... a kiddy-fiddler, that's one thing. World's a better place. But a sheila... shit.'

Roger stepped across and slapped him, a blow that made Gabrielle's own teeth rattle.

'Watch your mouth. My money's good enough for you, you've blown half it up your nose already. Well, do the job I paid you for. And take her where I can't see. If I got off on it, I'd have done it myself.'

Pigs, angry now, grabbed Gabrielle's arm in a grip that would surely leave bruises. She checked that thought. Bruises would be the least of it, unless something changed the outcome very quickly. She walked beside Pigs on still-spongy legs, trying to remember the self-defence course – make yourself a person, not a victim, don't let him dehumanise you, find some common ground.

When she thought they were far enough away from the others she said softly, 'He can turn nasty, that Roger.'

'Roger? Is that what he told you his name was?'

'Is he taking us all for a ride?'

'Not me babe, like he said, he paid up fair and square. More to come when we finish the job.'

'Kill me, you mean? Why would you do that? You don't even know me.'

'Nothing personal. Just a job.'

'It's personal to me. I don't want to die, I'm only thirty-six. I could still travel, enjoy my brother's family, have a child of my own, look after my parents in their old age.'

Thinking of Toby and Zoe and her Mum and Dad almost undid her.

'Do you know, my brother works in the hospital? He's the patholo-gist. If you kill me, it will be him that has to examine my body and find out how I died. Can you imagine that, his own sister?'

'They won't find you. Davey can dig a deep hole. They'll think you ran off to start a new life.'

Butterfly Soup

'Anyone who knows me, knows I like the life I've got. And they always find the body, especially round here where some family dog is going to dig me up over the weekend.'

Pigs yanked her arm. 'Shut up. He planned it, he knows his stuff. He's got a porn business that runs rings round the cops, he's smart enough.'

'If he's so smart, why's he having to get people killed? I thought the point of dealing in porn was to stay out of the way of the cops.'

'That's the thing that stuffed everything up. That Don got caught, didn't he? Fiddling with boys, the sick bastard. Then he's in jail, does all the courses and comes out a bloody convert. Ready to show the cops who the ring-leader is. So he's a kiddy-fiddler and a nark. Had it coming.'

'You don't have any time for men who abuse kids?'

'Can't stand them. Bastards ruined my life.'

'But Roger's one, he just said so. If I'm thirty years too old for him it means he likes six year olds. Why are you doing his dirty work?'

Gabrielle could feel Pigs processing this information. As the drug-induced clouds parted he stopped in mid-stride.

'For real? He told us he did adult stuff, movies for real men. No harm in that.'

'He wouldn't tell you the truth, would he? It just slipped out to put me down. But he hit you for saying "kiddy-fiddler". And why do you think he was mixed up with Don if he's not the same as him?'

She could feel him hesitating. His grip on her arm loosened as he tried to work this out. She tested her legs and prayed that they would hold her.

Pigs turned towards her. 'Shut up. You're trying to worm your way round me. He's got $10,000 with my name on it ...'

Gabrielle pushed him hard in the chest and ran into the trees. She could hear a thud and a yell as Pigs fell, but then blundering footsteps came after her. She zigzagged, trying to get deeper into the trees and let the darkness hide her. She stumbled over fallen branches and the soft pine needles doubled the spongy feeling in her legs, but fear gave her strength. After a while she paused and listened. She could no longer hear Pigs chasing her. That could mean that he had lost the trail, or that he was being cunning and had decided to move quietly. She hoped he would try to find her by himself, rather than admit to the others that he had lost her. As she listened she could hear the sea, so she knew where she was now. It was Rabbit Island, a popular picnic place with a long beach, set in a pine forest large enough to hide some evil secrets.

From the beach she would know her way to the road where she could find someone to help her. She turned towards the sound of the waves and moved softly through the trees, her ears scanning the darkness for sounds of pursuers.

At the edge of the trees she jumped down the bank on to the beach, then crept along, in a commando crouch, to where she knew the road turned towards town.

When she left the beach and stepped up on to the track she felt painfully conspicuous. Even though it was still too dark to see her watch, the grassy picnic grounds looked too exposed. Huddled under a tangle of tree roots at the edge of the sand, she groped in her bag for her phone.

As she held it, she wanted to dial but she was afraid Pigs might be near enough to hear her speak. There was a text from Martina, 'where R U?' She replied as quickly as she could, 'kidnapped rabbit island help me.' then switched the phone to silent mode and put it back in her bag. It had also shown her the time – four in the morning. She wanted to get away from this lonely place before the sun came up and let her be seen. Skirting round the picnic places she ran in loops to where the caretaker's cottage stood at the entrance to the park; she tried to remember whether there had been any signs of life when she had brought Lil to the beach.

Still crouched in the bushes, she heard a vehicle. As it came closer, she gathered herself, ready to jump out and flag it down if it seemed safe but her heart sank when she saw the white car seeking her like a predator. Pigs must have told the others and all three were looking for her now. She stayed very still as it went past, noticing only the driver. Roger, she guessed. Did that mean Pigs and Davey were tracking her through the trees? The car went round the barrier which was 'Locked in the hours of darkness', bumped through grass and low bushes and continued out on to the main road. Gabrielle allowed herself to breathe again and was about to run up to the cottage, when she saw lights coming back towards her – the vehicle had done a U-turn. She lay low, her heart pounding so loudly they would surely hear her.

The cottage was her best hope. When she could no longer hear the car, she crawled to the edge of the lawn, crouched like a runner and then sprinted to the back door. As she raised her hand to knock a pair of arms gripped her from behind, knocking the wind out of her.

'Got you,' snarled Davey in her ear. 'That was predictable.'

The breath struggled back into her lungs in gasps and she gathered herself to scream, but Davey put a hand over her mouth.

'No use yelling, there's no one there.'

His change of grip gave her a chance. Simultaneously, she bit hard on the hand over her mouth and elbowed backwards with all her strength, then ran for the shadows. Davey was still swearing as she slid deep into the scrub and lay very still. He blundered about for a while then his footsteps grew more distant as he worked his way back towards the beach.

The road was so near and the bridge lay ahead inviting her to cross but she was too afraid to come out into the open. She let herself down the rocky bank to the muddy estuary and set about crossing in the shadow of the bridge, painfully aware of each slurping footstep. Suddenly a beam of light caught her and she looked up to see Pigs leaning over the bridge, staring right at her. It took all her control not to scream as she stood, frozen in the mud, her eyes on his face. After a long moment, he jerked his head towards the road and switched off the torch. As his outline disappeared from the rail of the bridge, Gabrielle realised he was letting her go.

With a prayer of thanks, she trudged on. Mud squeezed up between her toes, soothing the cuts on her feet, and she wondered when she had lost her shoes. At the deepest point, the inlet was up to her thighs but she waded through until she could climb up the bank on the other side. She lay a few moments under the bridge, listening, and then, when she could no longer stand the inaction, she ran along the road and pushed through a hedge into a paddock. There was soft grass and the homely smell of cows. Checking her phone, she read the message from Martina: 'on our way + police' and almost sobbed with relief.

From behind the hedge Gabrielle listened for vehicles, wondering which would come first: the predatory one, from the direction of the park, or the rescuers from town. Now that she was still, the cold and shock gripped her so that her teeth chattered uncontrollably but she stayed where she was. Even when she heard the rumble of cars coming up the road from town she dared not expose herself until she was completely sure. When she burst through the hedge waving her arms, the cars halted with a startled screech. There were two police cars, followed by Kathy's ludicrous but so welcome Beetle. Kathy, Martina and Freda leaped out and ran up to Gabrielle, as Garth unfolded himself from the back seat.

The police quickly grasped that the three men were still in the park and since the only way out was over the bridge, they were trapped there, predators turned prey. As the patrol cars drove on, Gabrielle hugged her friends and looked towards town where the sky was growing blue with the first light of the morning.

Chapter Twenty-Two

They arranged themselves in the VW, with Garth in the front. It felt comforting to be snuggled in the back between Freda and Martina, warmed by their bodies and held upright in her exhaustion.

'He drugged me somehow. What do you think I took?'

'Probably GHB – gamma hydroxy butyrate.' Freda was knowledgeable in these things. 'It's used in drug rapes and there's been a bit of that happening locally. It leaves your system very quickly, so it's hard to detect. The police want us to take you to the hospital for some blood tests but they're not very hopeful that there'll be much left by now.'

'How did he get it into me?'

'Do remember what you drank with him?'

Gabrielle tried to think. 'We'd talked about it, hadn't we? How drinking from a bottle is safer than a glass and even more safe would be those boxes that you open yourself and drink with a straw. That's what I asked him for – apple juice, I even said the brand so that he would get it in a box.'

'Was that what you had?'

Gabrielle frowned. She tried to picture the box with the red apple, sprinkled with raindrops. It didn't come. She thought of the tall man handing her something with a smile. She tried to zoom in on his hand. A different box...

'He brought orange juice. He said they were out of apple. But the box was sealed, I had to really struggle to open it. I remember that because we made a joke of it. You know how those boxes can suddenly splurt all over your clothes. I was trying to be really careful and we laughed.'

Freda said, 'They use a syringe. It makes the drink look safe.'

Gabrielle thought again. 'He laughed a lot. I thought it was because he was friendly, but now it seems creepy. He was laughing because he knew I'd fallen for it.'

She was starting to shake again. Freda took Gabrielle's hand and held it firmly, saying to Garth, 'Tell Gabrielle what you did.'

Garth's big shoulders shrugged. 'I didn't do much. I wish now I'd done something sooner, eh? I was doing security duty at the club across the road so I saw you leaving Trixie's with that guy, looking as if you were really out of it. It seemed a bit odd, I didn't think you were the type to get smashed and anyway I'm pretty sure you're not into guys.'

In spite of herself, Gabrielle smiled. Outed at last!

He continued. 'I know the taxi driver, so when he came back to his rank I went across and asked him where you went. He told me the motel. It just didn't sound like you. Even if you were going to have nookie with some random guy, you've got a home of your own to go to. It was nearly time to knock off so I told my mate I was called away on family business and I went and got Kathy and these ladies and said I wasn't happy. They weren't happy either.'

Martina took up the story. 'So we piled into Kathy's car and went to the motel. We turned in to the street just as a white car drove out past us, but we couldn't see you so we thought nothing of it at first.'

Garth said, 'I was scrunched up in the back and could hardly see out, otherwise I might have recognised the guy who carried you out of the bar. But we missed that. What I reckon now is that Pigs and Davey had been watching you and when you went to the club they saw their chance. So this Roger did the set up, 'cause you wouldn't have gone with such obvious low-life as those two, and they followed in the car. Anyway, the light was on in the motel office so Kathy went in.'

Kathy took it up. 'The manager said no one of your description had checked in and she pretty much gave me the bum's rush. She said she'd had enough trouble for one night and she'd like to get some sleep. So we decided to drop Martina off at your place to wait for you and to call the police if you didn't turn up by morning. There didn't seem to be much else to do.'

'I sent you a text while Kathy was in the motel office,' said Martina, 'and it took a while but you replied before the others left your place so we called the police. They had had your call but didn't know where you were so they were quick off the mark when we explained.'

'Thank God, and thank you all, you've been wonderful,' said Gabrielle. Her mind flashed to the grave that was half-dug in the forest somewhere. Time enough to talk about that later.

The Beetle whirred steadily into town. First they dropped Garth off, then they went to the hospital where the blood test was quickly done. Back in the car, Kathy said, 'I need to get home. Jim will be horrified that I've been out all night. Where would you like to go now, Gabe honey?'

Freda said, 'Your place or mine?'

Gabrielle looked at the capable woman sitting beside her. She felt an urge to lay her head in her lap, to be comforted and cared for.

'Yours,' she said, 'that is, if that's ok.'

'Of course. I do perfect scrambled eggs and excellent coffee. Probably just what you need.'

Kathy dropped them off in a leafy side street, outside a tiny purple cottage. The door was only two steps from the footpath and Freda unlocked it, standing back for Gabrielle and Martina to enter. Inside, the cottage had polished wooden floors and a white floccati. Through French doors there was a view of a courtyard garden and the hills beyond, the eternal backdrop to Nelson. Freda pointed to a large armchair.

'Sit here a moment.'

She came back with some soft cotton trousers and a sweater and handed them to Gabrielle with a large ziplock bag. 'The police will want your clothes so put them carefully in there. Here's something a bit warmer to wear and the shower's through there.' She pointed to a panelled door. 'I'll start breakfast.'

The kitchen was a galley behind a bench. As she went through to the bathroom, Gabrielle could hear Freda and Martina talking softly.

She closed the door behind her and immediately her heart started thumping. The events of the night came back like a bad movie. She remembered how she had wedged herself against the door of the motel bathroom and tried to make her drugged brain think what to do. Suddenly her stomach lurched and she bent over the toilet bowl, retching. When the nausea subsided she washed her face and then sat on the toilet and tried to pee. For a long time nothing happened. At last the flow started, bringing relief. She straightened her clothes, washed her hands and looked at herself in the mirror: the pale face with violet shadows under the eyes was a ghostly version of herself. Mechanically she undressed, folding each garment and putting it into the bag. She stepped under the hot shower and scrubbed off all contact with the men who had rough-handled her during the night. She dressed in Freda's clothes, which were soft and warm, tidied her hair and then went back to the living room.

Freda looked up from the stove. She had changed into jeans and a checked shirt and looked tired and pale in the electric light. Putting a hand on Gabrielle's shoulder she asked with concern, 'Are you ok? You look wrecked.'

'I think the shock is hitting me.' Gabrielle felt wrung out.

'Eat something and then if you want to talk we're here to listen.'

Freda brought a small table over beside Gabrielle's chair and handed her a plate of scrambled eggs on toast. Then she poured coffee and set it on the table within reach. Gabrielle thought of childhood illnesses, when she would sit by the fire wrapped in her eiderdown and let her mother look after her. She gave Freda a grateful smile and began to eat, surprised at how hungry she was and how comforting the food felt. Martina took her plate and sat nearby, still unusually quiet.

Freda settled opposite with a plate and mug and began her own breakfast. Gabrielle became aware that there was some music playing. Recognition made her smile again.

'Satie's "Gymnopaedie",' she said, 'I love this piece.'

Freda nodded and smiled back at her. The three women ate quietly and let the slow sweet music flow around them.

After a while Freda gathered up the plates and refilled the coffee mugs.

'Do you want to talk about it?'

'I only remember flashes. When I used your bathroom just now I remembered how I shut myself in the motel bathroom and tried to think what to do. The worst thing was not being able to get my brain to work. Now I know how Lil must feel. I was like a hurt animal, just wanting a safe place to curl up in.'

'Your instincts were good, they got you through unharmed. You have to keep that in mind when you think about it.' Martina gave her the psychologist's reassuring answer. Gabrielle nodded; reassurance was fine but her main concern was to understand what had happened.

'Then when I thought someone had come to help me, it was those evil guys.'

Gabrielle began to explain what she had learned: that Don Lawson and Roger were connected in some way through child porn and that Roger had paid Pigs and Davey to get rid of Don. In doing so, they had set Jasmine up and led her to believe the crime was hers.

But when it came to telling what had nearly happened in the park she clammed up. It would be bad enough telling the police.

Freda saw she had come to a stop. 'I have to be at work soon so I'm going to try to get a little sleep. I'll drop you back home now. Then I'll collect Martina and take her to the airport on my way to the office.'

As Martina and Gabrielle got out of the car at Gabrielle's house Freda said, 'So I'll leave you two to talk.' She gave Gabrielle a smile, raised her eyebrows meaningfully at Martina, then disappeared down the driveway.

Once inside an awkward silence enveloped them. Gabrielle made tea and sat at the kitchen table where Martina joined her. She looked at Gabrielle over her cup, then put it down and cleared her throat.

'I'm so glad you're safe. It's been a worrying night.'

There was something else on Martina's mind. Gabrielle waited.

'I owe you an apology.'

A bad start. 'What for?'

'Well, two really. First, because you were right about your client. She didn't kill her father. And if you hadn't persisted, she would have confessed to the murder because she couldn't remember what she'd done under the influence of P. So I'm sorry I didn't take you more seriously and include what you knew in my assessment.'

Gabrielle nodded. 'Thank you. And the second one?'

Martina looked out the window and ran a hand through her hair. 'I should never have gone to bed with you on the weekend. It was impulsive and I wasn't thinking of the consequences for you.'

'I'm not sure yet what those are.'

Martina turned to face her, 'Well, maybe you want more than I'm able to offer.'

'What are you able to offer?' Gabrielle could hear her voice as if it was a long way away. She felt cold again in spite of Freda's clothes.

'I need to explain. Willa and I have been together for nearly seven years. We don't live together, she has her own house. We haven't always been monogamous, either. She's ten years older than me and she has a few exes she stays close to – mostly as friends. That's ok for the ones that I know, they respect our relationship. But recently the woman who was her first lover came back from England and I could see straight away there was something different this time. Willa got all secretive and unavailable, denied there was anything going on, then tore strips off me for being jealous. I said, fine, it's over then. The night of the dance was the first time I'd seen her for more than a month. She took me outside to tell me that Denise had gone back to England and there was nothing in it. I was still mad at her and said forget it, you can't just bring me back out of the box to fill the gap – I don't even want to listen to you till you're telling the truth.'

'So you took me to bed just to get back at her?' Gabrielle's face was hot and she could feel tears starting to spill over.

Martina groaned. 'It wasn't like that.' She got up and walked over to the window where she stood looking out at the leafless apple tree.

Gabrielle said, 'I feel such a fool. I've been attracted to you since we met and I thought you felt the same. You can't pick me up and put me down again just as it suits your plan with Willa.'

'That's why I'm apologising. I really do find you attractive and the way I felt that night was genuine, nothing to do with anybody else. But now, well, Willa doesn't want to lose me and we've got history together.

I think it gave her a fright to find I could leave her. It's not easy for her to be vulnerable, but when she came to talk about things last week I saw a side of her I couldn't walk away from. I've agreed to give us another chance, at least for a few months. I really am sorry if I hurt you, Gabrielle.'

'If!'

The tears were flowing now. Gabrielle took a deep breath and wiped her eyes on the soft sleeve of Freda's shirt.

'You have hurt me. You can't just play with someone like that. Maybe that's how it's done in the Wellington scene but I take relationships more seriously than that.'

Martina turned from the view and looked at her. 'Will you be all right?'

'I have to be, don't I? But I'm not going to help you to feel good about it.'

Martina said, 'I need to pack. Thank you, Gabrielle and I'm so glad you're safe. And you've saved your client, you did well.'

She held out her arms for a hug but Gabrielle stepped past her and shut herself in her bedroom. She was still crying softly when she heard Freda's car take Martina away.

Chapter Twenty-Three

The MG zipped along the highway. The sense of being low to the road and the throaty rumble of the engine were thrilling, even if it was too cold to have the top down. Gabrielle glanced at Freda who nonchalantly pulled out to pass a camper van and changed gear with a flick of her wrist.

'This is a very cool car,' said Gabrielle admiringly.

Freda grinned at her. 'I know.'

Gabrielle had been occupied for most of Friday, giving her statement and going back to Rabbit Island with the police. She had stood at the edge of the hole that could have become her grave, which they had found deep in the forest at the end of a rough maintenance track. In the autumn sunshine, among the sweet-smelling pines, the hole in the earth had looked innocent, like the beginnings of a fort that she and Toby might have made on the farm and roofed with an old piece of corrugated iron from Dad's shed. But the night-time landscape, in which she was hunted through the trees, stayed in her mind and disturbed her sleep.

So when Freda phoned on Saturday morning and suggested going for a drive she had jumped at the chance of some distraction. They were on their way to Blenheim.

As they slalomed through the hills of the Hira Forest, Gabrielle took the opportunity to debrief. Freda's sharp intake of breath as she explained about the grave in the forest said more than any words of sympathy. The lawyer had also had a busy day on Friday as she arranged for Jasmine to be moved out of the secure unit into the open ward, prior to going home. Understandably the young woman was shaken by everything that had happened and was taking time to adjust to learning that she had not harmed her father. Gabrielle tried to find out whether she nevertheless still felt responsible for his death. After all, she had led the murderers to him. But Freda found their client's closed face as difficult to read as ever.

They also ran through what would come next as far as the numerous charges the three men would face. Gabrielle would be needed as a witness, but that, Freda assured her, would be months away.

Gabrielle was relieved to leave behind the winding hills covered in dark pine forest, thinking that she might never enjoy a pine tree again. As the country opened out into dairy farms along a willow-lined riverbank, Gabrielle hesitantly raised the subject of Martina. She felt embarrassed to confess her hopes and disappointments to Freda but soon found that her companion knew quite a lot already and that she was acquainted with Martina from her regular visits to Wellington.

'It wasn't fair of her to capture your feelings like that,' she agreed, adding with a mischievous look, 'but if it broke the drought...?'

Gabrielle grinned sheepishly. She had a point.

The road twisted and turned as the landscape morphed into wine country. The neat rows of vines were losing the last of their leaves and the rose bushes, placed at the end of each row like wedding bows on church pews, had a few late blooms. The red, yellow and white roses against russet vine leaves with crumpled brown hills as a backdrop looked like a tourist brochure for Tuscany.

Deftly, Freda turned into a driveway and pulled up in front of a winery cafe.

'Lunch?' she suggested.

Gabrielle, who had hardly eaten since Freda's breakfast in the small hours of Friday morning, was suddenly starving. She nodded enthusiastically.

The room they stepped into had the happy hum of diners enjoying their food and wine. A log burner threw out a cosy heat and the wooden walls were like the inside of a barrel. A young waitress wearing a white blouse and black skirt, with a long maroon apron tied around her waist, showed them to a table and explained the menu. Outside the window, a lavender garden with clipped box hedges and pebble paths continued the Tuscan theme. Gabrielle felt herself relaxing as the nightmarish pine forest was eclipsed by the present grace and comfort.

Over lunch Gabrielle made a conscientious attempt to focus on the food, the wine and the very pleasant company. Reaching across the table she put her hand lightly on Freda's.

'Thank you,' she said, 'this is just what I needed.'

Freda smiled at her, her dimples creasing her cheeks.

Chapter Twenty-Four

Gabrielle walked up to the sliding door and knocked. Jasmine let her in. She had been released from the Unit and was back at her flat where she had agreed to see Gabrielle one last time.

There was a new toughness in her face. She met Gabrielle's eye and didn't use her long hair to hide her face.

Gabrielle could not avoid looking towards the doorway into the hall where there was a faint dark patch on the carpet.

Jasmine followed her gaze. 'Mum came round and cleaned up. I'm glad she thought to do that.'

'How has it been for you to be back at home?'

'Not as bad as I thought. I'm not going to be a victim any more. I just want to get on with my life.'

'What about Don? How are you feeling about him now?'

'It's weird that he's gone. I still don't properly remember that night.' She stared at Gabrielle, her face expressionless.

Of course she wouldn't want to remember; once she pictured the attack on her father it would haunt her forever. Better that the defence mechanism stayed in place. Or perhaps the drugs she took that night really had affected her ability to file those memories in any retrievable way.

'What did you learn about how Don died?' Gabrielle asked.

'They hit him in the face and stabbed him with my kitchen knife. I thought they were my mates. They said they would help me send him away. I thought they understood how I felt about what he did to me.' Her voice was faint, disbelieving. 'But they were just doing a job for some other creepy paedophile.'

She was quiet for a moment. 'And what if he was sorry? It would have made all the difference if he could have told me he had changed and he was sorry he hurt me.'

She shook her head as if trying to shake away the thoughts. 'He's not my problem any more. I need a new start.'

'Have you got plans?'

'The psychologist did my IQ for the court report. She was checking my memory to show the judge and that nurse, Penny, said the results showed that I'm quite bright but don't know much. I think that's what she meant. When I was a kid, I was too upset about Dad and too busy trying to look after Mum to pay attention at school. Penny said I should do a course.'

Good for Penny, thought Gabrielle. Beneath that forbidding exterior she had commitment to her patients.

Jasmine frowned. 'I don't know what course though. I've never thought about doing any better kind of job.'

'You know Kathy at the Women's Centre?' said Gabrielle.

Jasmine nodded.

'She could help you find something. I'm sure there'll be something that suits you.'

Gabrielle didn't know whether Jasmine would follow this up or not but it seemed like a way forward.

She continued with the words she had thought carefully about. 'I wanted to see you so that we could end properly. Endings are hard, often messy and not the way we thought they'd be. You and I were going along with therapy in a certain direction, then Don's death and the things that followed changed all that. It changed things for me too, so we are both different because of it and the same direction doesn't apply any more. I can understand that you don't want to continue therapy with me. I'm part of that messy time when everything got difficult, so when you put it all behind you, you have to put me behind you too.'

Jasmine was watching her face intently and seemed grateful for Gabrielle's words.

'So I just want to wish you well for the future and I hope things work out for you so that you can find something that you'll enjoy doing. I hope you can be the best of yourself.'

Jasmine stood up. 'I think I'll be fine. Thank you, Gabrielle, you helped a lot.'

She fished in her pocket and held out a round white stone. Gabrielle took it with a smile and closed her hand around it. It fitted neatly into the palm of her hand and felt warm and smooth.

'Take care,' she said to the young woman, then she walked down the path and got into her car. As Gabrielle drove away she could see Jasmine watching from the sliding door.